"Cover them good, partner," Pulovski said to the kid.

Pulovski headed toward Strom, preparatory to patting him and the others down.

Liesl looked over her shoulder—at Ackerman.

His gun was out, but he was shaky. His face twitched. He was aware that he was not the backup.

Liesl turned from the wall and headed toward him.

Pulovski, busy with Strom, glanced up sharply. "Shoot her, kid! Shoot her!"

Ackerman didn't know what to do.

"Stop!" he said. "Stop. Please, miss, I ..."

Pulovski turned to shoot Liesl and was kicked in the stomach by Strom.

Ackerman turned his gun to Strom but out of the side of his eye saw a lightning movement and heard a single word from Liesl: "*Amateur.*"

And then his gun was kicked out of his hand, her elbow was in his solar plexus, and he was down. Strom had already scooped up Pulovski's gun and ripped out the .22 from the ankle holster.

Ackerman looked at his gun, and made a desperate lunge for it ...

THE ROOKIE

NOVELIZATION BY TOM PHILBIN

Based on the screenplay by Boaz Yakin and Scott Spiegel

WARNER BOOKS

A Time Warner Company

For all the folks at Karl Ehmer's Quality Meats
in Huntington, Long Island, whose turkey sandwiches
have always been an inspiration to me.

THE ROOKIE

CHAPTER
1

OUTSIDE, David Ackerman knew, he looked fine. He had taken great pains with his appearance. His hair was cut short; he was shaved super smooth; his dark blue uniform had been pressed to perfection; he had polished each piece of brass individually, and had spit-shined his shoes. More, he was young—only twenty-six—and handsome, a dark-haired, dark-eyed man who could make women, young and old, feel a little funny when they looked at him. In short, he looked like he belonged in a recruitment photo poster for the Los Angeles Police Department.

It was the inside he didn't want them to see. The thing hidden there.

Everything seemed a little hazy, and slow, and he realized he was sweating, and that his heart was starting to beat a little faster. It was getting close to the time.

He blinked, tried to suppress the rising sense of panic.

Please.

"Next!" The voice came from inside the room and made his heartrate spurt. The voice was rough, cold, uncaring.

He stepped in.

There were three questioners in the room, two men and a woman.

"How long have you been on the job, Ackerman?" one of the men asked.

"Two years, sir."

"Speak up!"

"Sir. Two years, sir."

Then the other man spoke. He was worse than the first. His voice was low, judgmental, dripped with cynicism.

"You applied for detective in Burglary/Auto Theft. Why? Most of the young hotshots are lining up for Robbery/Homicide."

"Well, sir, I realize that. I figured there would be more openings in Burglary/Auto Theft and I could get assigned there more easily and get right into detective work."

"Tell me something, Ackerman," the second man said, "why are you on the police force?"

Ackerman sucked in his breath, swallowed hard. They might find out. God.

"I want to help people, sir."

Then a new voice, the woman's, much harsher than the men's, knifed in. "That's a lie, isn't it?"

Ackerman tried to speak, but couldn't. His heart started to beat even faster. He could feel it pounding in his ears, in his chest.

She spoke again. This time her voice was soft, deadly, the hiss of a snake.

"Do you have any siblings, officer?"

"No . . ." Ackerman managed. He felt like crying.

"You had a *brother*, didn't you?"

Involuntarily he started to tremble. He was sweating heavily. His eyes filled with tears. "I was just a kid, I . . ."

Then, he couldn't talk. He was suffused with sadness and terror.

"Help, Ackerman?" she said. "Help other people! *You murdered your own brother*, and you want to help peo . . ."

Then the men joined in, and they pounded at him, their voices strident, terrible, *knowing*. He wanted to beg them to stop. His heart was going like a triphammer, he started to scream, but it was a scream that made no sound . . .

Suddenly the scene was gone. He blinked. He was confused.

Where was he?

He was sitting up in bed, his body slick with sweat, his heart hammering . . .

He was in the bedroom of his house.

It had been a dream.

He became aware of a voice. It was his girlfriend, Sarah, sitting up beside him.

"Christ . . . David," she said, her voice heavy with concern. "Are you all right?"

His heart was starting to slow. He nodded.

"What's the matter?"

Without answering, Ackerman, nude except for briefs, got up and stood near the bed but facing away from Sarah, almost as if he didn't want her to see him.

"Nothing," he finally said, "just a little tense about that exam tomorrow."

"David . . . why are you doing this to yourself?"

Ackerman did not answer. He walked over to a dresser in a corner of the room. On it was a framed black and white photograph, a picture from long, long ago.

It showed two little boys in mock combat with swords.

Ackerman touched the picture, and tears came to his eyes. He felt so terribly, terribly empty.

CHAPTER
2

THE big, squat warehouses, located in the industrial area of Los Angeles, flanked the street as far as the eye could see. It was night. The sky was starless and maroon, almost black, a rain sky, the only light from a yellow street lamp about seventy-five yards down the block on a corner.

For the rat, a brownish-black Norwegian type weighing about a pound, hunched down near a curb gnawing on something, the ambience was perfect: not only dark, but dirty, damp, and apparently devoid of other life. The cuisine itself was four-star: a sandwich whose filling was unpoisoned peanut butter, its favorite, courtesy of one of the area workers who had dropped it there earlier in the day. In sum, except for the 750 times a year it had sexual relations, it was about as good as it got for the rat.

The rat would have been less pleased if it knew it was being watched intently from a darkened doorway directly across the street, some thirty yards away, by a big orange tomcat. The cat's amber eyes, normally slits in the daytime, were scarily dilated to the size of dimes and he could see the rat much closer and twenty times more clearly than human eyes could.

The cat was low to the ground, his body stretched out almost like a frankfurter, muscles tensed, a living statue, ready to charge . . .

The cat figured he had it made. Rats don't move too quickly, and its only escape route was a hole in a building maybe ten yards from its position. If the cat could think, he might think the rat was a dead duck.

Seconds ticked off, the rat gnawing, the cat just about to go when a sound came from far up the block, a low growl.

Cat and rat stopped, ears twitched, heads turned simultaneously toward what was perceived as a threat . . . maybe another predator. But so far the street was empty.

The growl shifted upward in intensity and it became clear something was approaching, and then light pierced the darkness and the thing turned into the street. It was huge, with shining bright yellow eyes. It was four blocks away and was moving closer.

Both creatures realized there was a decision to make, and both made the same one. The rat chomped down and picked up the sandwich and scurried toward the hole and the cat took one last rueful look at the rat and bolted out of the doorway in the opposite direction than the huge creature was coming.

The rat and the cat didn't know, but the creature wasn't alive, nor was it a predator. It was a car carrier. The predators were there—but on it.

The carrier squealed to a stop, its nose grill about even with where the rat had been eating the sandwich. It stood, engine idling loudly between the cavernous flanking warehouses.

In the cab was a driver and someone in the driver's seat. The driver was a slim man about forty with large, almost huge, sensual, dark eyes, a finely chiseled, spread nose, heavy lips, and black, short, collegiate looking haircut. He looked vaguely like the actor Peter Lorre.

He glanced at the Rolex he was wearing and spoke, his voice consonant with his appearance. The careful listener would have detected a slight German accent. His name was Erich Strom.

"Time. Get ready to secure our last three."

Strom was referring to the cars. Six Mercedes were on the carrier and he expected three more very shortly.

He was speaking to Loco, a solidly built Mexican who exuded menace and was aptly named. One look from Loco's black eyes could turn the stomach of most men to tapioca. Ironically, Strom was far more dangerous, not only because he was smarter and more devious but because he didn't look dangerous, like a Venus's-flytrap didn't look dangerous to a fly.

Loco opened the cab door and hopped down onto the street. He looked up toward the cars and made a motion.

Both doors of a white SL 500 secured near the front of the carrier on the top opened. From the passenger side came Ronnie Tersig, a thin, white-faced man of twenty-five who looked perpetually worried. From the driver's side stepped Harold Blackwell, a tall Texan with a very weathered face featuring crow's-feet lines that radiated back into his hairline. He had the face and eyes of what, in fact, he was—a pilot.

With an economy of motion based on lots of practice, Tersig and Blackwell climbed down off the carrier and went to the back.

Tersig gripped a handle and pulled it, activating a hydraulic system that lowered two aluminum ramps to the road. Blackwell then locked them in place.

Tersig gestured to Loco who gestured to Strom.

The men waited—Loco, Blackwell, and Tersig on the

street—all looking down in the direction in which the carrier had come.

Strom waited in the cab behind the driver's seat, looking straight ahead, occasionally glancing in the big side-view mirror up the street.

After two minutes he looked at his watch. They should be coming very soon.

Then he heard a squeal, and a car pulled into the block. Strom watched it and felt a quiet pleasure, a sense of fulfillment that was almost sexual.

It was a white Mercedes SL 500, sticker price of $83,500, that was the rarest of the rare. They were so desired that they were on sale used in the Los Angeles area for over $100,000. There was a six-month wait for them if bought new in the States, a six-year wait in Germany.

Strom smiled. And six minutes if bought from Erich Strom.

Inside the car, Strom knew, was Max, aka Maxwell Fenton.

The car—radio blasting rock music—pulled to a stop just before the twin ramps and then Blackwell and Tersig guided Max so he drove it up and onto the carrier flawlessly.

Max got out, his blond hair flowing, his eyes wild, thanks to the crack he had been snorting all day.

"One fucking SL 500 at your service," he said.

Blackwell managed a half smile but Loco was not smiling. He went over and walked around the car. "You scratch it?"

"No fucking way," Max said. "No fucking way." He knew that if he had, Strom would dock him at least a yard. But he enjoyed telling this big spic that he didn't.

Max beat a retreat into the darkness.

Angelo Cruz, a large Mexican with slicked back hair, stood on a corner a couple of blocks away and regarded the parking lot, which was directly across the street from a bank of classy restaurants.

Or, more particularly, one car in the parking lot.

He had been watching it for ten minutes, occasionally checking his watch. Since he had been there only two people had come out. *Bueno*. He would have no problem. Nobody better fuck with him anyway.

Like Maxwell "Max" Fenton, Cruz was known in the trade as a "puller" or "mule," someone who stole cars for a living—a good living at up to a $1000 per car—the first step in a chain that would ultimately deliver whatever he took off the street either to a chop shop, where its usable parts such as the rear quarters, nose, doors—anything without "VIN" or vehicle identification numbers such as the engine and transmission—would be cut up—chopped—and shipped to used auto yards for rebuilding other cars. Or the entire car would be put in a container and shipped whole to some foreign clime like Colombia or Argentina.

Like most pros, Cruz specialized, in his case Mercedes. Chop shops followed market trends, and Mercedes—particularly white, red, and black ones—were hot right now.

Cruz knew them inside out and there wasn't one made that he couldn't get in and be driving away in less than two minutes.

Cruz was proud of his work. Like this one here, this 340 SDL turbo sedan parked between the Jaguar and Nissan—he had done his homework. There wasn't a night went by when the restaurants didn't draw people with less than five or ten Mercedes. On a dare, Cruz figured he could empty the whole fucking lot of all of them in less than a half hour.

He was sure that when he came to pull one tonight he would.

Even if he got caught—who cared. Nobody, because stealing a car, unless you had a yellow sheet, was a Mickey Mouse crime that nobody gave a crap about. It was a sweet crime, low risk, high pay.

He glanced at his watch, which he had synchronized with Strom's.

2:02. He felt something surge inside him. Time.

He moved quickly toward the lot.

Three minutes later Angelo Cruz was cruising out of the lot with the car of his choice.

About three miles west of the lot where Cruz grabbed the 340 SDL, there was another parking lot, this one serving a nightclub.

The lot was packed with cars, all empty.

But the black Ford parked a half block away with a good view of the lot wasn't empty. In the front seat sat two detectives. In the passenger seat was Billy Parker and sitting behind the wheel was Nick Pulovski.

Pulovski and Parker were about as different as two cops could get. First, Parker was black, Pulovski was white; Parker had a family, Pulovski did not; Parker had a tire around his belly from home cooking; Pulovski had no fat at all thanks to hardly ever eating; Parker was large and friendly looking and hopeful; Pulovski was tall, lean, and hard, a middle-aged man with a chiseled, still handsome face that exuded cynicism. To Parker, it would all turn out okay. To Pulovski, life was a shit sandwich.

Yet both men shared something: they were cop partners, a relationship that got about as intimate as human relationships got. Lots of partners would say that they were closer to each other than their wives or husbands. Spend eight, ten, twelve hours a day with a person, sitting side by side, talking endlessly, sharing meals, standing side by side in a urinal, or sitting side by side in toilet stalls, and—the biggie—have your survival depend on your partner, you got close. Some cops said they even dreamt about their partners.

If a man and woman were partners, forget it. The divorce rate among female police officers hovered in the high ninety percentile. Sex had a way of following love and dependence.

And yet, to listen to Billy Parker and Nick Pulovski you would never know how close they were. Their affection was all below the surface, unstated, except in action when their asses were on the line, and one man would throw his life on the table to save the other's. Not that there was anything heroic about it. It was expected and done—and deeply appreciated.

But Parker and Pulovski—known in the squad room as Peepee—had something else to bind them. Both were in the Los Angeles auto theft squad, a duty that was widely regarded as a place mostly for cops who didn't want to be cops anymore. Cops who didn't like street work, or were trying to make connections for work after retirement, for cops who were afraid of violence, and, occasionally, for cops who screwed up. Though it wasn't one hundred percent true, it was almost always a place for cops without dreams.

Parker was there to make connections. Pulovski was there because he had never been good at taking orders. He always, as one CO once said, "gives you a little—or a lot—of shit. He doesn't obey orders, he's a pain in the ass, and he's crazy as a bedbug. And he fucking drinks and smokes shitty cigars."

For a long time now, Pulovski had been on auto pilot in investigations. He would spend most of his day doing paperwork, drowning his sorrows with a tin of cheap Scotch that he would swig in the men's room whatever chance he got.

Or, occasionally, they'd go on surveillances that often as not didn't achieve a single collar.

But not tonight. Tonight was special, the result of seven weeks of intensive investigation by him and Parker.

Little Felix, a pigeon he knew, had dropped him a solid

lead on Erich Strom, courtesy of another pigeon who was inside Strom's operation, and Pulovski had been scraping up money to pay Little Felix and his inside canary to develop the case.

And it had developed.

Pulovski and Parker learned that Strom operated at least six different chop shops in Los Angeles and he was a busy little beaver. Peepee couldn't get locations, but in time they would. For tonight, though, Artie, another snitch who was ripping off Little Felix, had given them something good.

"Tonight," Artie had told them, "they got a bunch of mules going out to round up Mercedes. And Strom's going to be in on it. I know one lot that's definitely being hit."

Now, they waited.

A clutter of coffee cups and a half-empty box of donuts on the dashboard indicated that they had been in the car a long time—four hours.

Nick sipped on a half-tepid cup of black coffee.

Parker turned to him and said, in his almost-girlish, chirpy voice he used when something surprised him, "Nick, how in hell can you drink so much coffee and not take a leak? You continue to amaze me. I've been to the bathroom once, and I know I'm going to use this bottle"—he referred to a capped quart jar one-third full of urine—"very soon."

"Every six months you ask me that, Parker," Pulovski said, his own voice, in contrast to Parker's, part whisper and part gravel, "and my answer is still the same. After twenty years on the job my kidneys have grown into one-gallon cast-iron containers. Better you ask why yours haven't developed."

Parker chuckled, shook his head. "There's only one Nick Pulovski."

"Yeah," Pulovski said, "and thank God you're not Fritz Friedhoffer."

Parker chuckled. "And neither are you."

Pulovski smiled . . .

Fritz Friedhoffer was a long-time squad member who no one wanted to go on stakeout with, at least not in a vehicle where there was no escape. He had very bad breath and his farts were legendary. One detective said, "Listen, Fritz's breath will only make your eyes water. His farts will make a pathologist puke."

Pulovski drained the last of his coffee—and both he and Parker were suddenly fixed on someone who had come out of the nightclub. He was a dark-haired, short Mexican dressed in what looked like a silk suit. Upon emerging he had checked out a couple of babes, then started to thread his way through the parking lot.

From time to time people had come out of the club, gotten in a car, and driven away. But there was a big difference between those people and a mule. This dude had a certain wariness, a studied nonchalance that experienced cops like Pulovski and Parker read instantly.

Plus, his left arm was stiff, not bending at the elbow. That's where he was holding the "slim jim," a narrow piece of sheet metal that would be especially designed to beat Mercedes power locks.

They watched silently, their minds working in tandem.

He went over to a black Mercedes 340 SDL that was parked about mid-lot and glanced around. Parker and Pulovski couldn't see what he was doing, but they knew that it was not legal.

After sixty seconds his head disappeared, and thirty seconds after that the Mercedes was rolling out of the lot. It turned up a street, heading away from them, then turned out of sight a block away.

"Let's get rolling, man," Parker said.

"Why the hell not," Pulovski, who had already started the engine, said. And with that he gunned the engine and the car bolted forward, spilling the empty coffee cups and donuts all over their laps.

Parker pushed the debris onto the floor. "Geez," Parker said, "I forgot that when I'm with you I have to wear my wet suit."

Pulovski smiled, then he didn't. He had stuck a fresh cigar in his mouth and then had pushed in the dash lighter. But it wasn't popping. Ten seconds later he pulled it out and tossed it out the window.

"Got a light," he said as he turned up the block the Mercedes had turned up and picked up its wedge-shaped taillights.

Parker, looking at the taillights, said, "Nick, there must be a hundred good reasons why you shouldn't smoke those things."

"Yeah, but right now," he said, also keeping his eyes fixed on the taillights, "I can't think of one."

CHAPTER
3

PULOVSKI'S idea was to stay within striking distance of the asshole they were following, but not so close as to take a burn.

At this time of night you had an advantage—maybe. The streets weren't loaded with vehicles, so you weren't going to get caught in a traffic jam.

On the other hand, you were more visible—much more. Traffic screened you. When the cars weren't there you were exposed.

Now, he had one car between him and the Mercedes.

Pulovski followed by feel: years of experience coming to bear in the moment. He reacted rather than thought. Later, if he wanted to pick it all apart, he would have seen the logic. But he was pure instinct now.

The Mercedes was picking up speed. Pulovski feathered the gas. The Ford was not souped up but Pulovski knew it could stay with the Mercedes unless it let it all hang out. That car had a chip in it to keep anyone from exceeding 165 miles an hour.

But Pulovski would have liked nothing better than a high-speed chase. Once, so long ago it seemed to him like it had occurred around the dawn of time, he had raced stocks on weekends. He had won some races and he still had the instincts, though not the reflexes, but he still loved speed; or, more to the point, activities where you walked a wire with your feet greased with Crisco and one slip would put you in intensive care or the bone orchard.

Subtly, the scenery was changing. The tail had run past high rises and elegant townhouses and condos and now the buildings got smaller, flatter, and less elegant. The Mercedes was on a due west track.

"He's heading for the industrial area," Parker said, plucking the thought right out of Pulovski's head.

He nodded.

Pulovski, who had remarkably strong white teeth for a man who smoked cigars and liked his grain, bit down a little harder on his unlit cigar and reeled in a little more of the invisible towline that connected the vehicles.

Everything was cool. He just hoped this asshole would not be stopped by some alert cop in a sector car. Just recently they had started profiling likely drug dealers or mules, and a Mexican driving a high-style car fit the bill. They called it a Valcary stop. They would be looking for drugs, but the end result would be to flush seven weeks of investigation down the toilet.

One good thing. The asshole was driving by the rules. He stayed within the speed limit and stopped at lights. And so far Peepee had not seen a single black and white.

Now, the driver stopped at a red light, and Pulovski eased off the gas.

It went green, and the driver made a right at the corner.

Pulovski followed, but the car that had been screening him went straight ahead.

Pulovski knew he had to be very careful now.

He knew that, whatever, he and Parker would have a short shelf life. He just hoped that it would be long enough.

Pulovski came to a light and eased through it just before it turned red and hung a right . . .

From nowhere another car was directly in front of them. Pulovski pulled the wheel hard right and the other driver went hard right and they avoided colliding by a hair and ended up parallel to each other. He glanced at the subject vehicle—it was stopped by a light—and then made ready to deliver an obscene broadside to the stupid son of a bitch driver of the other car . . . and the words died in his mouth.

The driver of the other car, a bright red 1963 Mercedes in mint condition, was a stunningly beautiful young woman with dark hair, dark eyes, and lovely features. She had fire in her eyes and Pulovski felt a warm sensation.

"Damn . . . feast your eyes on that," Parker said.

"She's a classic—don't make 'em like that anymore."

"Man," Parker said, "you've got tachometers for eyes, Nick. I was talking about the babe."

"So was I."

Pulovski smiled slightly at the babe and then tromped on the gas, the impression of those beautiful eyes seared into him. He bit down hard on the cigar.

At the pickup point, Erich Strom watched the rearview mirror as Cruz, in the second of the stolen Mercedes, approached the carrier. Without ado, Cruz drove the car up on the lower rack and Blackwell and Tersig chained it in place.

Cruz didn't stay to watch. He hopped off the carrier and he and Loco grinned at each other and then Cruz was gone away, like Max, on foot.

Erich Strom checked his watch.

A moment later, almost as if he could read his mind, Loco was there looking up through the open door at Strom.

"Morales is two minutes late," Strom said. "We're out of here."

Loco nodded. His brow furrowed.

"You shouldn't be getting your hands dirty, Angel Blanco. Too risky."

Strom's face smiled. His eyes rarely smiled.

"What, and miss all the fun?"

Loco grinned, then turned and headed toward the back of the carrier.

"*Vamonos*," he said to Blackwell and Tersig, who were on the street.

Tersig ran over to the hydraulic levers to activate them and retract the ramps.

But the sound of an engine made him hesitate.

It was Morales, approaching fast.

Morales pulled the car to a sharp stop just before the ramp, then drove into the last position.

"You're late, *maricón*," Loco barked. "*Get out of here.*"

Morales felt something squeezing in his stomach and made himself scarce fast as Tersig and Blackwell climbed up to secure the car.

In their own car, Pulovski and Parker turned into the street where Morales had turned and spotted the car carrier. The situation was clear. Both men tightened and a moment later they had a flashing red light on the dash and the siren hammering away.

Their approach turned Blackwell, Tersig, and Loco, who had joined them on the carrier, to statues.

Pulovski pulled the car to a halt a few yards from the carrier. Both men hopped out, sixteen-shot Berettas in hand.

"Freeze, motherfuckers!" Parker yelled. "Get your fucking hands up."

Parker, holding his gun in his right hand, held up his shield with his left. They approached cautiously. As a rule, car thieves were not dangerous. But investigation had shown these were not ordinary car thieves—and one could never discount danger.

Loco raised his hands slowly and Tersig and Blackwell, still on the carrier, did the same.

Pulovski walked toward them, gun and cigar pointed at them. He was smiling. "Little early in the season for Christmas shopping, isn't it? Who's in the cab?"

"Santa Claus," Loco said.

Pulovski responded by firing, the bullet exploding into the carrier framework perilously close to Loco—and one of the stolen cars.

"I don't believe in Santa Claus," Pulovski said with a low, ferocious intensity. "Try again."

The shot had cleared the air.

"*No one* . . ." Loco said, his eyes were blinking rapidly, "there's no one here but us, man."

Pulovski made an almost-imperceptible gesture to Parker, who immediately walked around past him, then slowly made his way up toward the cab on the driver's side.

The door to the cab was closed. Parker bent at the knees, tensed, and pointed his weapon at the door. He grabbed the door with his free hand and swung it open.

It was empty.

"Nobody here, Nick!"

Parker lowered his gun, closed the door.

Then, to his left, movement, substance. He turned and was looking down the barrel of one of the most feared weapons of all—a shotgun, this one twelve-gauge.

It occurred to Parker that the big-eyed dude holding the gun wasn't going to shoot. If he was, he would have.

If he did, *sayonara*.

Erich Strom pulled the trigger.

The blast was concussive, ear shattering, and threw

Parker back as if he had been picked up by a giant hand and tossed.

"Parker!" Pulovski yelled and in that millisecond of time Blackwell was into his jacket and pulled out a .357 Magnum, but before he could get off the first shot Pulovski was down on the ground, rolling, and the bullets started to kick up clumps of asphalt, and then Pulovski stopped, his gun up, and fired at Blackwell who, in one moment, pulled Tersig in front of him as a shield to take Pulovski's bullets, falling dead to the pavement, nothing to worry about anymore.

Then Pulovski rolled again, avoiding a new threat: Loco was also firing at him with a Magnum, kicking up divots in the road, inches from his body, and then he was behind his car, relatively safe.

He thought about what to do, and then he heard the big diesel engine roar.

Moments later he emerged—and saw the huge vehicle moving down the street, gaining speed, the still-down ramps sending up twin wakes of yellow sparks, and there, lying on the ground as if killed by it, was Billy Parker, face down as he had fallen.

Nick ran over, turned Parker over.

Parker had taken the full load of double-aught birdshot in the chest. There was a two-inch-diameter hole made up of a single hole one inch in diameter surrounded by nine more in a symmetrical pattern, each the equivalent of a .38 caliber slug.

Pulovski knew Billy was dead before he had turned him over. He had seen an exit wound in the back. The blast had traversed his body.

But he could not leave him lying face down on this street. Nor could he leave his eyes, now fixed and dilated, open. He used his fingers to gently bring the lids down.

"Hey, buddy," he said, "you never said good-bye . . ."

And there beside him was his peppered and bloodied shield

lying on the street. Pulovski picked it up and put it in his pocket.

He looked up the block. His face was racked with sadness but it gradually turned, turned to one filled with rage.

He started running toward his car.

CHAPTER
4

ERICH Strom made a mistake.

When leaving the scene, he could have easily gotten away by maneuvering the car carrier through the maze of streets down in the industrial area.

Instead, he headed for the freeway.

Pulovski had lost him but he took a chance and also headed for the freeway, knowing that he had just as good a chance of spotting him there as on one of the side streets.

Strom still might have made it, except for the access to the freeway. He had to bring the big carrier, which weighed 100,000 pounds, down to twenty miles an hour to make the long, laborious turn onto the road, and Pulovski, moving along at eighty miles an hour, caught sight of the rear of the carrier just as it entered the freeway proper.

Pulovski was at the access road in seconds and took it at close to sixty miles an hour, tires screaming, almost rolling over.

Traffic on the freeway was light, and within twenty seconds

Pulovski was directly behind the carrier, which was moving along at about eighty-five miles an hour, the ramps still down, bouncing and scraping and screaming, spewing sparks.

Pulovski slowed down, eyeballing the situation.

The Mexican was the only one he could see on the carrier itself. That meant that there were two in the cab, including the shooter. Three motherfuckers all told.

He bit down hard on the unlit cigar and tromped on the gas, pulling up to the right of the carrier.

Loco had spotted him and fired, just as Pulovski stomped on the gas and bolted forward.

The shot shattered his back window, and then Pulovski, driving with one hand, had his Beretta out of the window and was firing. Shots hammered off the frame and into one of the cars.

Loco, who had been between cars, retreated behind one of them.

Fuck, Pulovski thought, and dropped back directly behind the carrier.

The driver had his head out the window and was making some sort of throat-cutting gesture to the Mexican that Pulovski didn't understand.

But he understood who he had seen: Strom. He was the shooter.

Pulovski squeezed a shot off at him but the angle was impossible. He thought about driving up next to the cab but rejected it. He would be like a duck in a shooting gallery for the big Mexican.

For a moment the Mexican appeared—and then disappeared, seemingly under one of the cars. He wondered what the fuck he was doing.

Pulovski considered going up next to the cab, no matter what. He just wanted the joy of shooting at Strom.

Pulovski was about to do that when the meaning of Strom's

throat-cutting gesture became clear. The Mexican had freed one of the cars and it was rolling off the back of the carrier—at him.

Pulovski swerved left.

Most of it missed him. It clipped him a glancing blow in the rear end as it went by and he did a 360, his car at one point facing backward, watching the Mercedes smash into the rear of another car that also had swerved to avoid it.

Then Pulovski had it forward again, the only thing worse for wear his cigar, and was closing the gap.

Loco let another car go, but this time Pulovski was ready, and he easily evaded it and knew that there would be as many cars coming at him as were on the carrier. He was a ship, they were torpedoes.

Drastic fucking action was required. He took it, and inside the cab Blackwell, watching the action in the side-view mirrors, yelped: "Christ . . . who is this crazy motherfucker!"

. . . as Pulovski, demented, took aim at the ramps, skipping along at eighty-five miles an hour. He got one wheel on each and gunned the car up and onto the carrier.

Loco had been mesmerized by what he had seen and took no action. The *maricón* could never make it.

But he did.

Loco started to retreat to the front of the carrier. Pulovski squeezed off a shot.

"Come on, you lousy fuck! Come on!"

But Loco was out of sight and Pulovski stayed in the car to use the engine block as a shield.

He waited for Loco to appear. But he didn't, and then he went climbing up the ladder on the passenger side of the cab.

Pulovski couldn't get off a clear shot.

Loco yelled to Strom, "He's on the back . . . I've cut us loose."

Strom nodded. He was smiling, eyes included. "I know."

He glanced in the side-view mirror. He could see part of Pulovski's car and the ghostly image of his face through the glass.

He got a firm grasp on the wheel and then sharply turned it—with the desired effect. The cab went one way, and the 100,000-pound carrier, Pulovski aboard, the other.

"Have a nice day," Strom said.

In his car, Pulovski had seen the cab separate, and then he felt the carrier go nose down as it started to go. It had reduced its speed to seventy miles an hour. Pulovski waited to die.

The scene was almost surreal. The carrier was lying across the freeway on one side like a beached whale. A number of the cars had broken free and they lay askew all over the road with one resting on the divider, half on the road, half on one side of the freeway, half on the other. Smoke billowed up, but there was no fire.

Pulovski's unmarked car was crushed.

People materialized from nowhere, traffic stopped on both sides of the road. In the distance there was the sound of many sirens.

People were reluctant to approach the wreck, but then two young people did and were shocked.

From inside it all Nick Pulovski emerged, picking his way out of the debris, walking toward them with, crazily, an unlit cigar jammed in his mouth.

One look at his eyes showed that he was in never-never land. In fact, he was in shock.

The young people ran up to him.

"Hey . . . mister, do you need any help?"

Pulovski looked at them. He blinked. He was starting to go. He took the cigar out of his mouth, then looked at them.

"I could use a light," he said, and then his eyes rolled back into his head and he collapsed in their arms.

CHAPTER 5

AT around twelve-thirty in the afternoon, thirty days after he had been involved in the crash, Nick Pulovski entered the big gray building in which was located the precinct where he worked. He had a new unlit cigar in his mouth and he looked none the worse for wear.

But he was the worse for wear.

In the crash he had suffered a broken left collarbone, broken ribs numbers three and four on his left side, a jammed thumb, deep lacerations on his scalp that went to the skull itself, a concussion, assorted bruises all over his body, and, what he considered worst of all, a wrenched groin.

As he went down the hall, both uniformed and plainclothes cops greeted him, some telling him how sorry they were to hear about Billy Parker.

And some avoided his look. Some cops were superstitious. Talking to him might cause them grief. Well, he thought about those cops only one way: fuck 'em. Life sometimes meant looking at the inside of a camel's mouth, and if you

25

couldn't look for your friends and partners who the fuck could you do it for and what the fuck were you worth?

In the two weeks he had spent in the hospital, he did not think about Billy Parker much. It was part of living, and dying, and if you lived too much in the past it would destroy you. All you had was today, so fuck the rest.

On the other hand, he would not forget Billy. There were scumfuckers out there, chiefly Strom, who were going down, one way or another, because of it. That was for sure.

In fact, Billy was why he was back today—instead of thirty days from now as his doctors had implored him. And without wearing the sling for his collarbone, as he was supposed to.

"You're still a sick man," one had said.

"I've always been a sick man, doc."

The hall led to a large beige squad room filled with the desks of some of LA's finest plainclothes detectives, and some of its worst.

Pulovski's eyes immediately fell to two detectives, Lance and Wang, throwing spitballs at each other.

He smiled: business as usual.

Wang and Lance waved to him, as well as a number of the other cops, as he went by. He waved back, then went immediately into the glass-enclosed office of his CO, Lieutenant Ray Garcia, without knocking.

Garcia, a hard-looking middle-aged dude with dark, sad eyes and a weathered face, looked up from his desk.

"Hey, Nick," Garcia said, "good to see you up and around."

Pulovski stopped in front of the desk.

"Ray. I just spent the morning down at central records looking at mug shots. The guys on the trailer are there, the hump outside—Loco—and the hump inside, someone named Blackwell, an ex-CIA pilot gone dirty. Done close to three hundred mule flights over . . ."

"Nick," Garcia tried to interrupt.

"And Loco—Loco Martinez—he's got a yellow sheet as long as your arm, a very nasty dude . . ."

"*Shut up, Nick!*" Garcia interjected.

Pulovski smiled and shut up.

"You don't waste any time on polite conversation, do you, Nick? That's what I like about you." Garcia paused. "Either way," he said, "it don't matter anymore."

"What don't matter?" Nick said.

"The Strom case, because you're being taken off it. Homicide's catching now."

Pulovski's eyes narrowed. His voice lowered to almost a whisper.

"*Homicide?*" he said, as if the word had recently emerged from someone's ass. "Ray, the only way to get Strom is to bust him as head of his chop shop operations. Homicide'll just roast his flunkies and he'll walk away. I'm not . . ."

Then, noticing him for the first time, Pulovski took a hard look at someone else in the room, standing back in a corner.

He was a young, good-looking kid wearing a perfectly pressed suit and tie. A detective's shield was pinned to his coat.

"Who the . . ." Pulovski said, swallowing the obscenity before it left his lips. "Hey listen, kid, make yourself scarce, this is a private conversation."

"Uh, Nick. This is David Ackerman."

Pulovski's eyes widened in mock wonderment and appreciation.

"*David Ackerman?* Nice to meet you, David . . ."

Pulovski went over, a shit-eating grin on his face, and shook Ackerman's hand. Then he put his arm around his shoulder and escorted him through the doorway, closing the door behind him.

"Nick," Garcia said with a low menace in his voice.

Pulovski looked at him.

"That was your new partner."

Pulovski paused a millisecond. It was a joke, right?

"You're shittin' me," he said.

"Let him back in, Nick. *Now*."

Nick hesitated a moment, then went over to the door and opened it.

David Ackerman's eyes were shining, this because they were set in a face that was the color of a pale tomato. He came into the room.

"Don't mind Pulovski," Garcia said, "he's an asshole but you'll get used to the smell after a while."

"Flattery will get you nowhere, Ray."

Garcia's eyebrows raised. His tone was respectful, informative. "Listen, Nick," he said. "I went over Ackerman's test scores and records. The kid's perfect."

"Oh, yeah," Pulovski said, "then why's his shield on upside down?"

Involuntarily Ackerman's eyes dropped to his chest, and his face came up even redder than before. The shield was on correctly.

Garcia swallowed a chuckle and Pulovski, without further ado, went past Ackerman and out the door as if he weren't alive.

Pulovski threaded his way quickly through the room. Ackerman, feeling stupid and small, tried to follow.

Wang, of Lance and Wang, materialized beside Ackerman. Ackerman was acutely aware that faces all over the squad room were turned toward the little scene.

Wang patted him on the back, a welcoming gesture, but then handed him a Kleenex.

Ackerman took it but was puzzled. Wang explained, "Hey, kid. Looks like you forgot to dry off behind the ears this morning."

Lance, well named, materialized on the other side. He looked at Nick. "Be gentle poppin' his cherry, Nick. Some of these virgins bleed rivers."

"Kid," Pulovski said, "meet Cheech and Chong."

Pulovski started walking out of the room again, Ackerman trying to keep up with the hard-striding Pulovski and then someone in the room laughed—and the laughter continued to build with every stride Ackerman took.

The cause of the merriment was what Wang had put on Ackerman's back when he gave him a welcoming slap; a sign that said KICK ME.

Ackerman was super glad to exit the room, but just before he did Pulovski, who he had caught up to, reached across and delicately picked the sign off, crumpled it, and dropped it to the floor.

CHAPTER
6

TEN minutes after leaving Garcia, Pulovski and Ackerman were in a new black sedan parked, almost literally, at an intersection at Wilshire and Sixth. They had been sitting, locked in an immense traffic jam, for about five minutes, and there was no indication they were going to move.

Pulovski, who was driving, checked his watch.

"We have an appointment, or something?" Ackerman asked.

Pulovski did not reply. But he spoke to himself, out loud. "Fuck this shit," he said, and with that reached down and activated the siren and then manhandled the vehicle out of its lane and into oncoming traffic.

Ackerman could do nothing except wait to die, as cars coming the other way swerved to get out of the way, the siren and the unusual sight of a car bearing down on you for a head-on collision clearing the way like Moses did to the Red Sea.

The crisis lasted only a minute or so, and then they were beyond the jam and Pulovski kept the car cooking along at about eighty miles an hour.

Ackerman wanted to ask Pulovski where they were going but he sensed it was futile. And he was right.

Ten minutes later they were in Bel Air, the most upscale neighborhood in all of Los Angeles, a place where the help had better homes than most middle-class people. Rents started at about a million a month.

A few minutes after this they were tooling up the driveway of the equally posh Hilton Arms Hotel.

Pulovski, Ackerman saw, had very little patience for lines, so he drove past the Mercedes, BMWs, Cadillacs, Jaguars, and Rolls and the like that were lined up to enter the parking garage and pulled the car to a screeching stop in front of the carpeted entrance.

Pulovski got out and Ackerman followed totally mystified about what was going on and, not sure he was doing the right thing—but sensing Pulovski's urgency—pulled his gun from his belt holster.

"*What's going on here*?" he asked.

"You'll figure it out as we go," Pulovski said as he got out of the car.

Ackerman felt a surge of anger, but suppressed it.

Pulovski tossed the car keys to a stunned valet and walked toward the elegant front doors. Ackerman, still confused, holstered his gun simply because Pulovski hadn't pulled his.

He continued to follow Pulovski through the elegant lobby. He seemed to know exactly where he was going. Ackerman caught up to him.

"This is some kind of initiation stunt, right?"

Pulovski stopped dead and turned toward Ackerman. He grabbed him by the belt buckle, his face intense.

"Listen here, kid . . . the Jesse James look is out. You'd

better get a shoulder holster. Until then, conceal the weapon better . . .''

With that Pulovski pulled Ackerman's belt around so the gun, which had been hanging more or less over Ackerman's groin, was on the side.

"Besides, you don't want to be running around half cocked, do ya?"

Then Pulovski grabbed Ackerman's tie and loosened it.

"Another thing," he said, "the way you're dressed you look like an old fart. Now we're not UC but there's no fucking point in advertising to the whole world you're a cop. Put on something hip, young. Like you would normally wear."

Pulovski had added insult to injury.

"This is what I normally wear," Ackerman said angrily.

Pulovski shrugged, then turned, and he and Ackerman proceeded to the entrance of the open-air terrace restaurant.

The restaurant was elegance personified. The walls of the restaurant were actually elegant hedges, and there were flowers, greenery everywhere, including some that was interspersed among the tables. The fresh smell of greenery and flowers was tinged with the delectable smell of food.

Most of the tables were occupied; the people dining there looked very rich. And rich you had to be. Ham and eggs at the Hilton would set you back $25. A bucket of ice ("small") $7.00.

Pulovski scoped the restaurant. Ackerman got a sense he was looking for someone—or something.

Then the maître d' was there, looking at them questioningly. "You have a reservation?"

Pulovski held up his shield. "Yeah," he said.

"I see. Right this way, gentlemen."

"So that's what those things are for," Ackerman said.

"Never leave home without it."

Pulovski and Ackerman followed the maître d'.

"How about that table in the corner," Pulovski said.

"Yes, sir.

Ackerman and Pulovski proceeded toward it, and as they did a man sitting at a table adjacent to the one Pulovski and Ackerman were to be seated at glanced up—and did a double take.

It was Erich Strom. He was sitting with three other men, and there was one empty seat.

His face drained of blood and his eyes narrowed. For just a moment the snake had come out of the hole.

Pulovski walked up, his brow screwed up quizzically. "Haven't we met before?" he said, and smiled.

"I'm sure you're mistaking me for someone else."

Just at that moment Strom's waiter for the table arrived with drinks, one of which was a frosty mug of beer. Pulovski grabbed it and chug-a-lugged half of it. Then he pulled it away from his mouth, an expression on his face as if he had been drinking piss.

"Well," Pulovski said, "there's no mistaking these German beers . . . they always leave me with a bad taste in my mouth."

Abruptly he slammed the mug on the table. Silverware and plates jumped and beer splashed on Strom. Pulovski and Ackerman went to their table.

The three men at the table with Strom had been eyeing the little drama with high interest—and concern.

The dominant figure was Aldo Romano, a man in his thirties with styled dark hair and dressed in bright sports clothes that ran four figures and made him look like a pimp without a hat, and Sal and Vito, classic bomb throwers who were partial to black suits, black shirts, and white ties.

But Romano was not stupid. "Who the fuck was that?"

"Just a man with poor taste in beers."

"Don't jerk me off, Strom. You got your own problems, fine. But my people want their money. I don't get it for them, then I got fucking problems, *capish*?"

Strom *capish*ed. The wiseguys controlled all chop shop operations in the Los Angeles area—indeed in the entire country. If you didn't kickback a regular tithe or, like now, you didn't come through with a percentage of a deal they financed—as they had for Strom—you did have problems.

Strom's eyes flicked to Pulovski.

"I just lost a major payload, but my principal shops are still running. You'll have the money by next Friday."

Pulovski could not hear what Strom was saying, but he could hear a certain inflection in the tone that he liked. He knew Romano and the gorillas with Strom were wiseguys, and they weren't meeting to talk Little League.

The waiter strolled by just as Pulovski took out a fresh cigar.

"Hey, garçon," Pulovski said, "you got a light?"

"I'm sorry, there's no smoking here."

Pulovski groused and put the cigar away. Then he was surprised. The waiter was staring at the kid with his mouth open. Then he smiled broadly.

"Mr. Ackerman! It's been so long, I almost didn't recognize you. What a nice surprise!"

"Nice to see you, Walter," Ackerman said.

"Yes, how have you been?" Walter said, slipping his hand in his pocket. He took out a book of matches and lit Pulovski's cigar.

"Fine," Ackerman said, "fine."

"Good," Walter said, then put the matches on the table. Then he noticed: no ashtray.

"I'm so sorry . . . one moment, I'll bring you an ashtray, sir."

Pulovski looked at Ackerman after Walter left. "What the hell . . . you used to work here or something?"

"Not exactly," Ackerman said, a smile playing around his mouth.

Pulovski was still curious. "What gives?"

"You'll figure it out," Ackerman said, "as we go."

A minute later Walter brought the ashtray followed by their waiter, who brought menus.

As they looked, the girl who almost collided with Pulovski as he trailed the Mercedes was walking along on a hedge-flanked path that led to the restaurant another way.

Then she saw Pulovski, tensed, and stopped. Strom, who she was late meeting—fortunately—had described the crazy cop who had trailed the car carrier—and they both assumed he was dead. It had to be more than coincidence that he was here.

She backed up and left. She was sure Pulovski had not seen her.

In fact, Pulovski had not noticed her. He was too busy examining the menu and marveling at the prices.

He sucked on his cigar deeply and appreciatively, the clouds of smoke wafting upward. He knew Strom was in some pain.

He smiled. "Well, kid, since you're so popular here, why don't you order."

"You want the best?" Ackerman said.

"Why the hell not."

Ackerman handed the waiter the menus back without looking at them.

"We'll start with the Beluga caviar, then we'll have two orders of the lobster thermidor."

Pulovski watched the kid and his eyes widened again. But he recovered quickly.

"And bring a bottle of that fancy-assed French champagne, will you?" Pulovski said.

At Strom's table, the waiter approached. The waiter looked very unhappy. He stopped, leaned down, and said to Strom softly: "I'm very sorry, but this card has been declined."

Some of the color went out of Strom's face; his eyes flicked to the wiseguys.

He reached into his jacket pocket, withdrew a wallet, then picked out and handed the waiter a Carte Blanche card.

The waiter shook his head slightly. "We don't take Carte Blanche."

Strom lost his cool. *"You'll take what I give you!"*

Pulovski had heard this exchange. He loved it. He got out of his chair just as the waiter arrived with the bottle of fancy-assed champagne.

"Come on, kid," Pulovski said. He walked over to Strom's table. The waiter had left to get the manager.

Without preamble Pulovski planted his cigar in the middle of what was left of Strom's lunch. Pulovski's eyes were blazing. He spoke with jaws clenched, low, whispery, his mouth hardly moving.

"It's too bad you're not who I thought you were. If you were, there's something I wanted you to have."

Pulovski reached into his jacket and threw Billy Parker's peppered, bloodied shield on the table. "That comes with a price, motherfucker." And then he turned and started out, Ackerman beside him.

The maître d' stopped him. "Excuse me, sir, what about your bill?"

Pulovski looked back at Strom. Their eyes met. "That gentleman over there said he would cover it." Then he was walking out again. He could feel Strom's eyes burning into his back. And Romano stared equally hard at Strom . . . just as Pulovski had hoped he would.

CHAPTER
7

DAVID Ackerman and Sarah were in the bedroom of his modest bungalow house in Hollywood. They were in bed, but very much awake, and had been there for a while.

After an hour of almost violent sex with David, Sarah's slim, lovely body was bathed with sweat, her lustrous dark hair hanging down as limply as it got when she took a shower.

David was inside her. She was sitting astride him. They had both just orgasmed again.

She looked at David, whose handsome face was covered with a fine down of sweat. She leaned down and kissed him.

"God," she said, "I love you."

David looked back. He said nothing. It triggered something that had been bothering her not only during this, their latest sexual encounter, but for weeks. The quality of the sex was wonderfully satisfying, but only on a physical level. There was something missing, something emotional. Not from her.

From him. It was almost as if his body was making love to her but his heart was somewhere else.

She lifted herself off him and sat near him on the bed. He had not moved.

She looked at him again. She felt a fluttery feeling in her stomach. Something was wrong, very wrong.

"David," she said softly, "where are you?"

"Right here," Ackerman said.

She shook her head. "No . . . wherever you are you haven't been here for a long time."

David got up and walked across the room. There was a mirror hanging on the wall adjacent to a dresser.

He looked at himself in the mirror. Sarah watched him. He seemed to be searching for something in his face. What?

Finally he spoke.

"Back when we first met, you must've thought you were hooking up with someone who had it all going for him . . . now you're finishing law school and here I am, an auto theft cop in scenic Los Angeles."

"I have no regrets, David. And I have always supported every decision you've made. Christ, David, when you finally do make one it's a minor miracle."

Ackerman turned from the dresser. He looked at her. "I see all those guys around you when I pick you up after class . . . all those fucking together guys with together lives. I don't know why you stick with me."

Sarah got up and walked over to him. She slipped her arms around his neck. Her eyes searched his.

"I know that whenever there's something important, you always tell me . . . and I love you for it. But something's going on now, and you're not telling me . . ."

Ackerman paused a long time before speaking. His eyes were indescribably sad, tormented.

"I don't know what it is. Something's going to happen."

"What?"

"I don't know. I . . ."

Sarah said nothing. She let her eyes do the talking.

"I just feel I'm going to fail . . . again . . . like I . . ."

Abruptly Ackerman stopped.

"What?" she gently urged. "What?"

"I can't talk about it. I . . ."

Blessedly, the phone rang. He went over and picked it up. It was Pulovski.

"Hey, kid," Pulovski said, "be ready in half an hour. We're going on a little trip."

Ackerman might have felt anger in another situation. Now, he just felt relief.

Sarah watched him head toward the bathroom. Her eyes were full of pain.

CHAPTER
8

ACKERMAN was standing outside his apartment waiting for Pulovski a half hour after the call.

He tried to turn off the conversation that he had had with Sarah, but couldn't.

Yes, he could fail again. He had tried to be in his father's business and quit that. He tried post-graduate school—and quit that. He had tried a dozen other jobs—and quit. He had had many girlfriends—and the relationships all ended in tears and torment.

He always blamed himself. He had been failing people since he was very, very young.

But the cops. Maybe, he had thought, being a cop would be something special. Make him feel good about himself . . .

He had always admired cops. Admired their bravery.

So, despite deep fears, he had gone on the job and had done very well as a patrolman, though he was assigned to a low-crime area and never, really, had been tested.

Then, because of his record and test scores, he had a chance to become a detective. Of course he couldn't bring himself to seek an elite assignment, like homicide. Auto theft was more his speed. A job where he wasn't likely to be tested, but it was better than nothing . . .

He tried to force himself to stop thinking—and was successful.

Pulovski, the usual unlit cigar jammed between his teeth, pulled up to the curb in a black sedan a half hour later, and Ackerman just knew there wouldn't be an apology. He hated it.

They drove in silence for a while.

"Where are we going?" Ackerman said.

"You'll see when we get there."

A fuck you surged inside Ackerman but he suppressed it. Pulovski made him feel like such a rookie . . . lower than a rookie. No. It was just the way he felt about himself.

"What's the complaint?"

"Strom. What else?"

"The loo said we were off that," Ackerman said, using the slang name cops used for lieutenant. "That homicide was catching."

Pulovski turned toward Ackerman. Pulovski's face was a mask of scorn. His cigar seemed like some dark accusing finger.

"Hey, kid. Be fucking real. My partner was put in a hole not too long ago by that scumfucker. There were at least three people standing by that hole—his wife and two kids—whose lives would be changed forever by that. You think what Garcia said to me is going to dissuade me from certain fucking actions. Do you think Garcia thinks it will stop me? If you do, you go get a brain transplant."

Ackerman said nothing. He felt small—and stupid.

* * *

They had been traveling through the middle-class communities of West Los Angeles, a place mainly comprised of modest homes . . . a typical suburb in a big city.

But twenty minutes later the scenery took a turn for the worse. They were moving through East LA, a flat area lined with small, run-down houses fronted by dirt yards, and equally flat buildings, many covered with colorful graffiti, some of it mindless moronic meanderings but some artfully done.

The people on the street were strange. Young, old, whatever, they stared at the car when it went by. In other neighborhoods people would go about their business. Not here. Here they watched you. Everybody watched you . . . fearfully, it seemed, or with anger. Christ, any car that went by was a threat.

"Welcome to drive-by country, kid."

Ackerman said nothing.

"Never worked East LA, have you?"

"I've never been to East LA."

Ackerman wondered how he would handle things if he got involved with some of the bad guys who lived—and died—here. He did not want to ponder that too long. It did bad things to his stomach.

Ackerman had stopped and picked up a box of donuts and coffee. Pulovski, eyes on the road, flipped the lid up and extracted one.

He glanced at it and looked at it as if he had just selected something from a cat litter box. But it was merely a donut, albeit a fancy one with pink frosting and peppered with sprinkles.

"I always wondered who ate these fucking things," Pulovski said. He tossed it out the window—one guy made him smile when he ducked—and searched for and extracted a plain one.

Ackerman said nothing for the moment. It seemed his conversation with Pulovski consisted of either absorbing barbs or asking questions. He asked a question.

"Listen . . . at the restaurant today . . . we obviously weren't there for lunch. Who was that guy? Was that Strom?"

"Just someone I ran into a while back."

"How did you know he was gonna be there?"

"That's my job."

"Well, that's just great. You know I'm supposed to be your partner . . . what about my job?"

"What about it?" Pulovski said, taking a big bite out of the donut.

Ackerman bit his lip so hard it hurt.

Ten minutes later Pulovski pulled the sedan to a stop outside a large warehouse, one of a number in the area, which was also dotted with junkyards or, as they advertised in the Yellow Pages, places where they sold used auto parts.

They walked inside. Or rather, Ackerman followed Pulovski in.

The main floor was large and filled with vehicles, most of them new and expensive, in various stages of repair with hoods up; a couple were on lifts. A number of mechanics were working on cars.

Pulovski seemed to know right where he was going. Ackerman followed him about midway on the floor to a Lotus, which was painted a bright fluorescent green.

Someone wearing protective gear, his long blond hair flowing down the sides of it, worked on one of the wheels with an arc welder.

Pulovski waited until the mechanic, unaware of the detectives' presence behind him, turned off the torch, and he could be heard.

"Want to know what a real criminal is, Ackerman?" Pulovski said.

The blond-haired mechanic turned at the sound and pushed up his black protective visor.

"The son of a bitch," Pulovski said, "who painted this car, now that's a criminal."

The blond-haired mechanic was Max, the same Max who stole one of the Mercedes—unknown, he prayed, to Pulovski—the night Parker was killed.

He wiped his hands on his greasy overalls. He was very nervous.

"Mr. Pulovski . . ." he said, "what are you doing here?"

Pulovski, Ackerman noted, acted as if Max didn't exist. He stepped over to the car and ran the tips of his fingers over the hood.

"Anyone," he said, "who would deface a work of art with a color like this ought to be shot."

"I've only been working here three weeks, man. I don't need no trouble."

Pulovski scanned the shop. He knew there was little or any chance of IDing any hot metal here. The VIN numbers would have long been removed.

"Well, Max, that's why I'm here. To keep you out of trouble. Rumor has it you're running with a pretty fast crowd these days. I just thought I'd remind you how short your legs are. You're going to fall behind the pack. You'll get eaten."

Max's face was the picture of aggrieved innocence.

"I haven't let you down, man. I've been clean for a year, so you can stop lookin' over my shoulder."

"Okay, Max," Pulovski said, "don't make me lose my faith in humanity."

Max nodded. He wished Pulovski would leave. But Pulovski didn't.

"Looks like you're getting your paws on some fine machinery here. I'm glad for ya. But if anything comes in that looks like it's not owned by the particular person, you give me a holler, huh?"

"You know it, man."

Pulovski turned to go. He was, he thought, not the only one who had little faith in humanity. When he had first entered the warehouse he had noticed, in a far corner and almost out of sight, the eye of a TV camera. Somebody, somewhere in the building, could be seeing and listening to it all.

In fact, Erich Strom and Loco were.

Both men were standing before a bank of a dozen black and white TV security monitors that showed various areas of the three-story building. They had heard the entire conversation, and Loco was reacting to Pulovski's comments about the gaudily painted car, which happened to be his.

"You hear that motherfucker talk about my car?"

"Put it back in your pants, Loco. He was being kind."

Loco and Strom eyed Pulovski and Ackerman as they headed out of the shop.

Loco waited until they passed out of the field of vision of the camera, then trotted toward the front of the room they were in. The wall consisted of frosted glass segments—small windows. Loco opened one and looked down past the lower roof of an adjacent warehouse.

Pulovski and Ackerman got into the car. Loco's face was pale with rage.

CHAPTER
9

THE scene was classic: Los Angeles at night as viewed from a hill. Lights spread as far as the eye could see in the center of which were boxy office buildings, ribbons of moving lights on the roads, and, far in the distance, a big plane, red lights blinking, approaching Los Angeles International Airport. It was a scene that had been repeated ad infinitum, perhaps ad nauseum, in the innumerable movies that were made in the city.

Nick Pulovski hardly noticed nor did David Ackerman. They had just gotten out of the car and Pulovski was looking down at a bar in the foreground, and Ackerman was looking at him. Ackerman, per usual, was pissed.

"This isn't our complaint. I've been chasing around after you all day . . . what the hell are we doing here?"

Pulovski, as usual, did not answer—at least not right away.

He had a slight smile playing around his mouth as he scoped a flat, one-story structure at the bottom of a hill with a lighted sign outside it: "La Casa Blanca," which literally meant white house but that had, someone once said, "nothing to do with the white house and nothing to do with purity."

La Casa Blanca's clientele was indicated by the assemblage of vehicles parked outside. They were mainly motorcycles, but there were also a lot of pickup trucks and one or two older cars that looked like they had been taken out of a local junkyard for a night on the town.

Salsa music pumped through the darkness, and the bar seemed to be filled with red light. It spilled out of the barred windows and a window in the battered front door giving the ground a weird reddish hue.

Then the music got temporarily louder as the door opened and a man was half carried out by a large bearded man, through the door, thence to be kicked to the ground. The bearded man growled something and disappeared back into the bar.

Now, Pulovski answered. "This," he said, "is where the fun starts. Some nasty people frequent this establishment. C'mon, kid."

They picked their way down the hill and, Pulovski leading the way, went into the bar.

Ackerman was assaulted by the smell, a noxious blend of shit, piss, vomit, sweat, marijuana smoke, and disinfectant.

Almost all the lights were red, but Ackerman could see, and what he saw made his stomach tighten.

The place was filled with badasses, mostly Mexican bikers, bandannas on their heads, their arms heavily tattooed—including the women—and many had that special sheen that indicated that soap and water was not a priority in their lives.

They all seemed to be looking—at him. Ackerman tried to control the tightness and wished that he had worn something more in keeping with the place. He hoped they would leave soon.

"Buy yourself a drink," Pulovski said, "and watch your ass, 'cause if you don't somebody else will."

Then, without further ado, Pulovski left and headed toward a hall that apparently led to a back room. Ackerman had a feeling akin to what a little boy might have when left by his mommy in a department store.

Ackerman swallowed and stepped up to the bar, squeezing between two bikers, both dressed in jeans, leather and chains, and filthy bandannas. They were ripe.

The large, bearded bartender, the same guy who kicked the patron out, came up and stood in front of Ackerman. He had the butt of a cigar clamped in teeth that had gone through various stages of yellow and were now beige. He had little pig eyes, maybe blue, but hard to tell. Ackerman wasn't being too observant.

The bartender blew a cloud of smoke in Ackerman's face. The smell was not as bad as a guinee stinker but close. He suppressed a cough.

"Yeah?" the bartender said with a voice about three years away from throat cancer.

"A beer please."

Christ, he hoped Nick would hurry.

Pulovski was down in the relative coolness of the basement and it was packed with people, mostly Mexicans, yelling and screaming, and surrounding a plywood ring from which was issuing some horrific gnashing, growling sounds. Two pit bull terriers, the most ferocious dog known to man—a dog that would, experts say, give a mountain lion pause—were fighting to what would be, one way or the other, the death. One would kill the other in the ring, or the loser, if alive when he left the ring, would be killed by the owner: owners of pit bull terriers did not eat defeat too well.

Pulovski pushed his way through the frenzied mob. He was looking for someone. The someone, a small, ratty-looking Mexican with thinning hair, had spotted him first.

"Oh, shit," he said beneath his breath, and then stepped into a doorway, hopefully out of sight.

A minute later the man, whose name was Little Felix, felt a viselike grip on his shoulder. It was Pulovski. He looked at Little Felix like he had recently emerged from an enormous nostril.

"Hey, man," Little Felix squealed as Pulovski pulled him out of the doorway and then down an adjacent dark corridor, "you can't come here. You're crazy."

Pulovski waited until they were all the way down at the end of the corridor before speaking.

"You're going to give me the name of the canary at Strom's, so I can deal direct, or, Little Felix, you're gonna be in a world of shit piled so high you'll be looking down on the fucking stars!!"

Little Felix was a tough street guy. He could take a trimming. He had been worked over by experts, and he had done some bits. Fuck Pulovski, he thought.

"If I'm paid," he said, his dark, liquid eyes a blend of defiance and supplication, "I'll trade."

Pulovski hesitated. He tilted his head slightly, his eyes narrowed. "Okay, Little Felix, let's see what we got."

From inside his jacket he pulled out a clear zip-top plastic bag plump with white powder.

"I don't expect you to give me a name for nothing," Pulovski said.

Little Felix's tongue ran across his lips. His eyes were riveted to the bag. He nodded and reached for the bag.

Pulovski smiled slightly. "First," he said, "the name."

Outside, in the bar, a couple of minutes after Pulovski exited the room, one of the habitués of the place emerged from the bathroom. It was Loco Martinez, and he spotted David Ackerman right away. The fuzz with the pig who dis'd

his car at the warehouse and who they tried to whack on the
car carrier.

Loco went up to the bar and, leaning between Ackerman
and the biker to his right, bumped into him. The bartender
and Loco exchanged smiles, and then Loco backed off.

Ackerman had no idea what was going on. He did know
he didn't like it.

The bartender put a bottle of Pabst in front of Ackerman.
"Two bucks," he said.

Ackerman reached into his back pocket . . . his wallet
wasn't there. With a rising sense of panic, he searched his
other pockets. Nothing.

"Two bucks," the bartender rasped.

Ackerman was about to start explaining when a sharp whis-
tle, off to his right, interrupted him—and everyone else.

Loco was standing by the bathroom, holding Ackerman's
wallet in his hand like a prize fish.

"You tell your partner," Loco said, "Loco was here. You
got that, boy?" Loco pocketed the wallet and headed for the
door.

Ackerman stepped forward. "Come back here!"

Ackerman made a move toward his gun. "I said sto . . ."

A nearby burly biker grabbed Ackerman's hand and twisted
it, sending shooting pains up Ackerman's arm, forcing him
to the floor, and then the bartender came around from the
bar, whacked him in the head, and he went down, and then
he was engulfed by bad guys who started to randomly knock
the living shit out of him.

Within thirty seconds he was bloodied, near unconscious,
and two of them lifted him to better work him over and were
just about to when a voice boomed from near the bathroom.
It stunned everyone and they turned.

Pulovski was standing there, his shield in his left hand,
his brow furrowed, his face sincere.

"This is a crackdown, assholes!" he said, letting that sink

in. "Everyone in this fucking place driving without insurance is hereby under arrest!"

The crowd was silent, confused. Insurance? Most of the people in the room had only felony beefs.

Then someone got it, and tittered, and soon the room was engulfed with appreciative laughter.

Pulovski leaned down and helped Ackerman to his feet. Pulovski was his usual caring, compassionate self. "You should've told me," he said, "you like group sex, kid."

Ackerman looked and felt like he had been in a fight with a grizzly—and lost. Pulovski led him to the door. Before they reached it a demented voice cut across the room.

It was the voice of Little Felix. He was holding up the bag of powder Pulovski had given him.

"This shit is talcum powder, you double-crossing gringo pig bastard!"

"Yeah, but it's top quality," Pulovski said, and he and Ackerman were gone.

CHAPTER
10

ACKERMAN decided it was fruitless to ask Pulovski where they were going, and, when they arrived, why they were there. Why should Pulovski deign to tell him anything? He was only his goddamn partner.

Fortunately, he knew where they were. They had pulled up across the street from an auto junkyard, one of about twenty he had seen in the area. Some areas of Los Angeles, like any big city, had certain areas devoted to certain things like restaurants, theaters, diamonds, the garment district, etc. This area was devoted to used auto parts.

There was a series of pole-mounted lights within the interior of the yard, which was fringed on top with vicious concertina wire, which was about ten times as nasty as barbed wire.

There were, no doubt, junkyard dogs.

They got out of the car and approached the yard.

Ackerman, his face now starting to seriously swell and feeling the aches from the shellacking he took, felt terrible.

Pulovski noticed. "What's the matter, kid, those donuts aren't agreeing with you?" he said, smiling.

Ackerman couldn't even answer.

Pulovski stopped at the entrance. "I'm goin' in. You watch my back . . . think you can handle it?"

Ackerman was mute. Pulovski shook his head and moved away just as the pole-mounted yard lights went off. Suddenly the yard was in complete darkness and the small mountains of flattened cars, which occupied perhaps seventy-five percent of the yard, were silhouetted blackly against the sky. Ackerman, who had started to move into the yard, looked at them. They seemed very threatening. He had to get a hold of himself.

Ackerman moved cautiously. He could not see Pulovski. The only real sign of life was from a shed, about fifty yards away, with a light in a window.

The light went out.

He paused.

Ackerman could not see him, but a man emerged from the shed. It was Morales, the mule who had stolen the 340 SDL from the parking lot across the street from the nightclub.

Just a half hour earlier he had been in dirty uniform and gloves, but now he had taken a long hot shower and was all duded out in a white silk suit, which had set him back $2000, or what he got for two cars.

He got into a spanking new blue BMW parked outside the shed. It was his car, perfectly legal. The frame, tran, and engine were from a salvaged wreck, the rest of the parts he had personally stolen himself, and the VIN numbers transferred to it. A cop could look up his asshole with a microscope and find nothing.

Tonight he had nothing on tap—except a date with a soft broad named Minnie whose nickname was Ears. He was looking forward to that.

He put the key in the ignition and turned on the car. It

hummed to life. He gave it a little gas and put the car in gear when he heard the crane starting up and was just about to investigate when something smacked into the roof and Morales felt his stomach traveling toward his throat.

The car was rising, fucking rising. What was going on?

Pulovski was going on. He was sitting in the squarish cab of the crane, a fresh unlit cigar jammed in his jaw, and he was deriving great pleasure from watching the BMW—Morales acting like a trapped cockroach inside—going upward.

Ackerman was close enough to watch the scene, and despite the swollen lips he smiled and winced and . . .

Suddenly there was a sound behind him that he knew what it was instantly but didn't want to turn. It was the low growl of a dog, a *deep* low growl, meaning it was a big dog: chihuahuas don't growl deep.

He turned and it was confirmed: a rottweiler, which a dog trainer his father knew named Captain Haggerty described as a Doberman with a glandular condition. He weighed about 125 pounds. His baleful eyes stared at him from a massive head, huge teeth bared, drool hanging from a slack lower lip.

Ackerman farted and felt a fullness in his bladder.

He was only vaguely aware of the BMW rising . . . and then as the rottweiler appeared to be about to jump, Ackerman, now completely without pain, started to run, very aware that he could not outrun the dog that he heard behind him, and then, with a prodigious leap born of pure terror that had its origins in some slimy Neanderthal bog, leapt up onto a car and started to race from car to car, the rottweiler not able to get at him, but indeed hoping that he would make a misstep.

Pulovski, meanwhile, had raised the BMW to eye level—his eye level some twenty feet off the ground.

Morales eyed the ground, yelled to Pulovski.

"Hey, man, what the fuck are you doing?"

"I had a talk with Little Felix. I'm the cop that's been

footing your bills, scumbag. You and me are going to make us a little arrangement."

"I don't deal direct with no pigs."

For a moment Morales's head disappeared—and when he emerged he pointed an automatic out the window and fired. Pulovski ducked—and yanked the control sideways, sending the BMW smartly into a stack of flattened cars, jarring his gun loose.

"*Jesus and Mary*," Morales said, "*my fucking car*."

"Listen real close, asshole. I've got enough shit on you to send you away to Q on a nice long holiday where one of the studs who pump iron all day will be calling you honey within a week. From now on, like it or not, you're in my direct employ."

Morales looked at him. He didn't know what to say. He had been to the joint once and he knew one guy who went in straight and came out a flaming fag who had to wear suppositories to hold his shit in . . .

Meanwhile, Ackerman had gained on the dog—he was now a full car length from him, and then he saw the solution—an empty, battered old station wagon with the door open, and on the far side of where the dog was . . .

He jumped down and in seconds was in the car and closed the door behind him. He had beaten the dog, which slammed its drooling mouth against the closed passenger side window passionately. Ackerman was sweaty and scared, but he felt good . . .

He took a deep breath, contemplated his next move . . . when he became aware of a sound. Snoring? Breathing? Someone with emphysema? What?

It was coming from behind.

He turned and looked. A second rottweiler was in the process of opening its eyes, Ackerman having had the profound bad luck to have roused it from its slumber . . .

Morales, meanwhile, had concurred with Pulovski's proposition.

"Okay," he yelled, "put me down, man!"

Pulovski slapped the control lever and Morales and the BMW went down and bounced off the ground like a ball, only without the resiliency . . . and then Pulovski heard shots, two, and he was out of the cab, his Beretta drawn, running toward the source . . .

The scene stopped him short. He felt a profound sense of merriment.

Ackerman, a few yards from a battered station wagon, was in a modified Weaver stance, his automatic leveled at two rottweilers that would obviously like to rip him a new asshole but were not pursuing the matter.

Pulovski deadpanned it.

"Good work, kid. Now read 'em their rights."

CHAPTER
11

AFTER they left the junkyard Pulovski said he would drop Ackerman off, but on the way Ackerman started to feel even more of the effects of the trimming he took in La Casa Blanca. As it happened, Pulovski's place was in West Los Angeles, on the way to Ackerman's place.

"I have just the thing to fix you up, kid," he said.

Five minutes later they were in his very modest house and Ackerman was leaning over the toilet bowl throwing up.

After it was over, and he had washed up and carefully blotted his swollen face with a cold dishrag, he felt a bit better. So when he emerged from the bathroom he stood in the doorway and noticed, for the first time, that there was no danger of Pulovski winning the Homemaker of the Year Award.

Both the couch and upholstered chair were worn at the edges with stuffing showing through, the walls and ceilings were dingy, the paint peeling on the ceiling. There was clothing and assorted papers and magazines scattered around, empty and partly full glasses resting on most of the flat surfaces, dishes piled in the sink, pots and pans on the stove, and near the sink, across the room on the kitchenette linoleum, where Pulovski was pouring out a couple of Scotches at a corner of the counter he had cleared away, there were five or six mashed cigar butts.

Indeed, the place smelled like a cigar butt.

"What a dump," Ackerman said.

"Don't brag about it, kid, just shut the goddamn door."

Ackerman half smiled and walked across the room. As he did he noticed some old black and white photos, brownish and curling at the edges, taped to the walls.

He stopped and looked. They were of Pulovski from years ago in various racing scenes, at a pit stop, posing near a stock car, another with a group of buddies, three showing him holding trophies, and one—the only one with a woman in it—showed Pulovski in racing gear, helmet in one hand, holding a pretty young woman around the waist.

Pulovski had sidled up to him and handed him a glass of Scotch. He quaffed half of it—and started to cough up a lung. After a while he got control of himself.

Pulovski looked at him.

"You got suckered tonight, kid. And it ain't gonna be the last time. Only difference is at some point you're going to start learning to be prepared."

Pulovski walked away and put his foot up on the edge of a table that looked like it had been beaten with a chain. He pulled a pants leg up and removed a .22 ankle holster, then rubbed his ankle.

"You still race?"

"Only on the freeway."

Pulovski took a cigar out of his jacket, peeled the cellophane, and placed the cigar between his teeth.

He ferreted through his pockets for a lighter—unsuccessfully of course.

"Shit . . . kid, you got a light?"

Ackerman shook his head.

"See, what did I tell you about being prepared."

Pulovski went over to the stove. He elbowed a big pot off one of the front burners. He tried a knob, got nothing, then tried another.

He kicked the stove.

"Fuckin' gas company."

Ackerman, now the experienced drinker, quaffed the rest of the Scotch without going into a coughing spasm. Pulovski headed back toward him.

"Looks like you won some races," Ackerman said.

"Ah, local gigs—strictly small-time."

Ackerman gestured to the photo showing Pulovski and the pretty young woman.

"Your wife?"

"Ex-wife."

"What happened . . . she didn't like racing?"

"Nah . . . she loved racing. She just hated me."

"What, uh . . . what . . . do you mind telling me what happened?"

"Yeah," Pulovski said, "I do. I make it a policy never to play my old movies. They all have lousy endings."

They were quiet for a moment. Pulovski sipped his drink, savoring it. The last time he coughed because of whiskey was when he was five.

"You got someone?" Pulovski said.

Ackerman lowered his eyes, reddened a little.

Pulovski loved it. He smiled broadly. "Looks pretty serious, kid."

Ackerman squirmed a little more—and Pulovski's smile turned to a guffaw.

After he stopped laughing, he said, "C'mon outside, kid, I'll show you the rest of my estate."

The backyard was an extension of the apartment, a mini junkyard with a number of cars on blocks and in various states of disrepair. Tools, predictably, were all over the place, mostly on the ground.

Ackerman stepped in front of a vehicle that looked like it had taken direct mortar fire.

"This thing has seen better days," Ackerman said.

"Yeah," Pulovski said, "well, so have I. I just tinker with these babies to let off steam . . . always was better at driving 'em than fixing 'em."

Ackerman only half noticed what Pulovski said. He eyed a vinyl tarpaulin, covering something.

Pulovski yanked it aside and Ackerman smiled with pleasure. It was a streamlined motorcycle brilliant with chrome, in perfect condition, and it seemed terribly out of place.

"Sportster 1965," Ackerman said, "she's a classic."

"You know your bikes, kid."

Ackerman approached and ran his fingertips over the glossy gas tank.

"I ain't sure what's wrong with her, but she hasn't been starting up lately," Pulovski said.

"You have the key?" Ackerman asked.

Pulovski bent down and took a key out from under a brick and handed it to Ackerman.

Ackerman stuck the key in the igniton and turned it. The lights came on, but the engine didn't start.

"What'd I tell you?"

Ackerman nodded, preoccupied, and picked up a screwdriver off the ground.

He unscrewed the headlight, found a small electric socket—and reconnected the wire that was loose. He put the key back in the ignition and turned. It roared to life.

"Good work, kid," Pulovski said, "now you can get started on the rest of these."

Ackerman smiled. "Can I ask you a question?"

"You're always asking me questions, kid."

"Why," Ackerman asked, "don't you answer my questions?"

"No need. You'll learn as you go."

"It would be nice to know before I go where I'm going."

Pulovski took the cigar out of his mouth.

"Okay, kid," Pulovski said, "let me just tell you this one time. You saw me with that asshole hanging like a fish at the junkyard?"

Ackerman nodded.

"He's a canary, kid, and that's how most police work gets done. Canaries. Snitches. We pay them money, or give them other things, or give them deals—there are dudes out there who will roll over on their mothers rather than go to the joint. We pay 'em, we work 'em, we sometimes knock the living shit out of them. It's deals, kid. Deals. Police work is contacts and deals. Do you think I'm Sherlock Holmes and you're Dr. Watson?"

Pulovski smiled.

"Now this Morales, he sang a nice song tonight. And over the next few days Strom is going to feel like he had his chute packed with a Louisville slugger. And that's exactly the way I want it."

"What did he tell you?"

Pulovski went back and poured himself another drink.

"Hey, kid," he said, "one day at a time. What do you want—all my secrets?"

And he threw down the Scotch.

CHAPTER
12

THREE days after Pulovski indicated to Ackerman how most police work was conducted, Erich Strom was sitting on the couch of his glitzy, expensive apartment in North Hollywood, watching the news on television. Liesl, the woman who had narrowly missed colliding with Pulovski and narrowly missed being seen by him at the Hilton Terrace Restaurant, was standing nearby, also watching.

While Erich Strom was not physically feeling like he had a Louisville slugger jammed in his chute, figuratively he certainly did.

On the screen was a pretty Oriental reporter named Connie Ling. Standing next to her, a cigar in his mouth, was Nick Pulovski, going through his usual ritual of trying to find a light.

In the immediate background, looking uncomfortable, but more suitably dressed in casual clothes as Pulovski had suggested, was David Ackerman.

The camera panned to the right, and suddenly a parade of shackled people, led by plainclothes as well as uniformed cops, were leading people out of an auto parts yard to a waiting van.

Ling spoke as images filled the screen, mainly of cuffed people being led out of yet other junkyards and garages.

"I'm standing in front of an East LA garage that is the latest link in the chain of almost half a dozen chop shops busted by the LAPD in the last three days."

She turned her attention to Pulovski.

"This is auto theft detective Nick Pulovski," she said as Pulovski was still trying to find a light.

"Detective Pulovski, you seem to have gone very much out of your way to insure that we were here for these raids."

Pulovski looked very serious.

"Well, ma'am," he said, "it's always the homicides and splashy robberies that make the headlines, and it's about time this kind of crime gets the attention it deserves . . . it's the greatest crime against property there is.

"Now we realize that since it is such a high-profit, low-risk crime it's impossible to make a real dent . . ."

And then Pulovski warmed to his task, making the reporter look very embarrassed and requiring some judicious bleeping of what Pulovski was saying, which nevertheless could be made out by anyone . . . "but it is possible to hurt the individual *bleep bleeps* (scumbags) who are taking advantage of everyone else. I happen to know a particular *bleep bleep* (asshole) who is responsible for this whole *bleeping* (fucking) operation . . ."

And then he looked into the camera, his eyes narrowed, his lips curled.

". . . and that *bleep* (son) of a *bleep* (bitch) is out there hurtin' . . . he's hurting and I *bleeping* (fucking) like it . . ."

Strom used a remote to turn the TV off.

He and Liesl sat in silence. There was steam in the room.

Then: "If I could afford it," Strom said, "I'd blow a hole through this fucking thing."

He paused again.

"This," he said, "is a very dangerous man. He has forced us into a very difficult position, and we're going to have to make some moves we didn't anticipate. And there are a few ends for us to tie up. Okay?"

"Whatever you say, Erich, I'm with you."

CHAPTER
13

ON Friday night, the day that Strom was to make payments to Romano, a new black Porsche moved slowly down a long circular ramp and came to a stop in a dimly lit, low-ceilinged garage, the third level down of a three-level facility where the cars were mostly parked for long periods while owners went out of the country or were otherwise occupied. A few of the cars were covered with tarps.

It was a perfect place for a clandestine meeting—only one way in or out and you could hear someone coming—and that was why Romano chose it for his meeting with Strom. If he didn't have the money, they were prepared to deal with him.

Romano had gotten increasingly nervous when he had seen that Chink reporter on the previous night with that cop who fucked over Strom in the restaurant. Those had all been Strom's chop shops. If he was hurting for bread before, what could be the story now?

Romano had neglected to tell anyone above of the trouble

he could be having with Strom. If he did, he could get into bad trouble himself. If he had to tell someone, he would have to tell them, but he wanted all his ducks in a row.

Romano was sitting in the back of the Porsche. Vito, one of the people who had been in the restaurant, was driving. Sitting next to him in the passenger seat was Sal. They were loaded for bear and, perhaps appropriately, were dressed in black.

For a moment Romano saw no one, and then he saw something that triggered a warm feeling. Strom, an aluminum suitcase in hand, had emerged from behind a car and was walking toward the Porsche. Walking next to him was a big spic who, in fact, was Cruz.

Strom stopped after a few yards and waited until the Porsche pulled up to him and came to a stop.

Vito turned the car off and he, Sal, and Romano got out and stood opposite Strom.

Strom looked happy, a slight smile on his face.

Romano was pleased too, but he wouldn't show that. You never want to show these humps anything they can use against you.

"It better be here, Strom," Romano said, "I came prepared."

As he said it, two other Mafioso emerged from near the ramp. They walked up to join Romano, Sal, and Vito.

Strom continued to smile slightly.

Romano saw nothing that was dangerous.

He set the suitcase down on the concrete and opened it.

For a moment he smiled and then recoiled in disbelief. The suitcase was filled with newspaper.

He looked up at Strom but at that moment, coming from the ramp end of the garage, a horn blared loudly. Instinctively, all the Mafioso, including Romano, turned.

A millisecond later Strom had dropped to the ground and Cruz was on one of the new dudes and had drawn his stiletto

deeply across his throat, severing his carotid artery and jug-
ular and sending arterial spray everywhere.

Vito, Sal, Romano, and the new wiseguys went for their
guns, but none noticed that Blackwell had slithered out from
under a car, twelve-gauge pump shotgun in hand. He started
to blast away, the sound of the reports deafening in the con-
fines of the garage, and a moment later Vito had part of his
head blown off and the second new wiseguy hit the concrete
like a sack of potatoes, part of his chest wall missing.

Sal had his gun out and fired a shot but was momentarily
distracted by something and then was blinded by the lights
of an oncoming Mercedes that slammed into him and tossed
him like a rag doll, with just as much life, onto the concrete.

Now, only Romano was left. Blackwell approached with
a shotgun, and Cruz, his stiletto dripping blood, stood near.

Romano never carried a gun because it was a felony to
begin with and as an ex-con he would be doubly liable.
Anyway, who needed a gun with four buttons with you?

Now, he had nothing to protect himself. His life was in
Strom's hands.

Romano, backlit by the lights of the Mercedes, stood in
front of Strom. Romano's lips trembled. He hadn't prayed
in years. He started silently saying the Act of Contrition.

Strom, the same slight smile on his lips, looked at him.
"Romano," he said, "you don't know the meaning of being
prepared."

Then he casually raised a .38 and squeezed off a round.
Later, Cruz would have to throw out his shirt because he
couldn't clean the dura matter off that had sprayed on it.

Killing had a sexual edge for Strom, something he had
discovered when he had first killed when he was all of ten
and living in the Reperbahn, the red-light district of Hamburg.

A john had been with his mother, then had told him that

he wanted to buy him an Italian ice. Would he like to take a ride.

Strom said okay.

But the john took Strom to a deserted area of the city and raped him, and warned him not to tell anyone.

Strom said he wouldn't and then the john, who was drunk, had fallen asleep and when he awakened—feeling something warm on his neck and chest—realized that his throat had been cut. The sight of the man dying was like seeing a porn film to Strom, who reveled in the man's mouth opening and closing like a fish out of water, trying to breathe, and shortly thereafter Strom had introduced himself to the joys of masturbation, recalling those potent images as he hammered himself to orgasm.

He had told Liesl about the showdown with Romano and had told her that they would have to be moving on, but that he had a plan to get them a nest egg to take with them. And they had to leave. Wiseguys didn't like it when you clipped other wiseguys, but most of all they didn't like not being paid.

Now, he was in bed with Liesl and she was moving rhythmically under him and he was hard as blue steel even though it was their third time in less than an hour.

Liesl liked to kill, too, Strom knew. He had watched her do it a number of times, and after he had told her about his confrontation with Romano she had pressed him for all the gory details. And, at one point, furious urges had built in both of them, and they were soon on the bed, their bodies squirming and bucking against each other to relieve the beautiful pressures.

Now, they orgasmed together, and then lay down side by side. Both knew that the night was young.

Only one thing interfered with Strom's enjoyment. The continuing image of Pulovski. He was a fanatic, and therefore a very dangerous man.

CHAPTER
14

I T was night and the driveway, lined on both sides with
lights and relatively straight, ran through acres of mag-
nificently manicured land. The driveway looked almost
like an airstrip. Indeed, a small plane could probably have
utilized it very easily.

But a driveway it was, and now it was jammed bumper to
bumper with a long line of expensive cars such as Mercedes,
Rolls, Jaguars, Ferraris, the cars of wealth and prestige, and
all were heading toward a magnificent-looking cream-colored
house that was actually longer than the driveway and con-
tained forty rooms, all of which looked like they were home
magazine pages come to life. Perhaps one detail said it all:
the bathroom faucets were made of pure dull gold and were
worth $7000 each.

If wealth was power, the man who owned this house was
not to be trifled with.

David Ackerman and Sarah looked bizarrely out of place.
Though Ackerman was dressed in a suit and Sarah a party

dress, her dark hair up and her makeup subtle and impeccable, the transportation was offbeat. They were on a Kawasaki 750 bike, David driving, Sarah's legs clamped around his back, and both wearing motorcycle helmets. Ackerman was tooling up to the left of the traffic approaching the house in the right lane.

Sarah could feel the tension pulsating through Ackerman's body.

"Come on, David," she said, "it won't be so bad."

"Sarah, if I die and go to hell it's going to look exactly like my parents' house."

Sarah said nothing, but wondered. If he hated it so much, why was he here?

Ackerman asked himself the same question and got the same answer. Guilt. That's why. It was his mother's birthday, and as much as he despised helping her celebrate it, he couldn't stay away.

As they got closer, the couple could hear the soft jazz floating out the windows and open doors.

Valets, in formal wear, their shoes shined to a high gloss, helped the arriving VIPs out of their cars and carefully herded them through the doors.

Ackerman didn't have to look to know what kind of people were going to this birthday party, but as he parked near the front and came to the door, he did. They wore their wealth on their bodies, almost as if if they died at the party, they could take it with them. Women, tanned and with smiles worth at least $20,000, were given to low-cut gowns and jewelry and rings on all their fingers. They used makeup like clay.

The men, equally tanned and with expensive, toothy albeit false smiles, were given to pinkie rings.

"Christ," Ackerman said, "what would these guys wear if they outlawed pinkie rings."

Directly inside, greeting the guests, was the birthday girl

herself, Laura Ackerman, a formerly beautiful blond woman with a hard-chiseled, wrinkled face and eyes, Ackerman noted as they approached her, that were red and watery . . . not because she was sentimental about her birthday but because she had, as usual, been snorting cocaine.

For just a moment Ackerman felt a dip of sadness and recalled ever so briefly some long-gone day when she was young and beautiful and she had held his hand and . . .

The sadness turned to anger. Anger. That's what he felt toward both his parents practically all the time.

"Happy birthday, Mrs. Ackerman," Sarah said, giving her a little hug.

"Don't remind me. Sarah, you look *gorgeous*."

She leaned over and kissed—the air. Her sense of distance was not the best. She made a move toward David but he stepped back, easily avoiding her.

"Those allergies have been acting up again, huh, Mom?"

Mrs. Ackerman blinked and looked hurt. The remark had cut through the cocaine.

Ackerman looked at her and felt a surge of sadness. He leaned over and hugged her and kissed her.

David and Sarah proceeded to the edge of the dance floor where Sarah was promptly pounced on by an older man who asked her to dance. She agreed, and David watched her as she started to dance . . . and noted with interest that at least one of the other men dancing nearby tried to brush up against her. Whatever, he thought bitterly, turned you on.

He got himself a glass of champagne and shortly there-after was spotted by a group of his father's friends—and flunkies—and started to make mindless conversation. They had, he figured, about as much real interest in his life as the man in the moon. They only talked with him because of some notion that being friends with him would mean they were friends with his father who, it was rumored, did not own "half of Los Angeles at all. No more than a third!"

As he—or they—spoke he glanced idly through the screen of gyrating dancers—and got a shock. The tall figure of Nick Pulovski, beer in hand, cigar jutting from his mouth, relatively spiffily dressed, was standing there.

Ackerman approached.

"Nick . . ." he said when he got close enough. "Nick!"

Pulovski turned around as Ackerman came up to him.

"I didn't know we were on a first-name basis, kid."

"Why . . . what . . . are you here to bust my mother for substance abuse?"

Pulovski smiled, his eyes narrowed.

"That's funny. The real question is: What the hell are you doin' on the job? Christ, you've got so much going for you . . . your uncle was just telling me you almost got degrees in engineering and econo . . ."

Ackerman bristled.

"Do I have to hear this shit from you too?"

"Lighten up, kid, enjoy the scenery. Check that out," Pulovski said, glancing toward the dance floor, "over there . . ."

Ackerman followed Pulovski's view. It was Sarah, dancing with another middle-aged admirer.

Ackerman turned back toward Pulovski.

"Look," he said, "who invited you anyway?"

Someone behind Ackerman answered.

"I did, Davey."

Ackerman turned. It was his father, Eugene, a good-looking man with leathery skin and graying hair, a man who exuded power.

He put his hand on David's shoulder.

"My son doesn't talk to us, Mr. Pulovski. If I hadn't seen your terrific X-rated performance on the news I would never have known who his partner was."

Ackerman stared at his father, barely able to control his anger. He turned and walked away. He just knew that his father had something on his mind. He rarely did anything that was spontaneous.

"Let's take a walk," Eugene said to Pulovski.

David Ackerman went to the refreshment table and picked up a drink. He sipped it and watched his father and Pulovski as they headed toward the patio. Then Sarah was beside him, and gripped his arm.

"C'mon, David, let's dance," she said. Reluctantly he put down the drink and went with her.

Outside, Eugene Ackerman walked Pulovski to the pool, which was the size of a small lake.

Ackerman sipped from a glass of champagne, and Pulovski sensed that he was concerned about something. Ackerman looked up at Pulovski.

"Mr. Pulovski . . . you look like a man who likes to get right to the point, so I'm going to be very direct."

"Why the hell not," Pulovski said.

"I've always given David everything he needed . . ."

He paused, then continued, "But he won't take anything from me or his mother anymore . . . it's like he's completely cut us off . . ."

He stopped, took another longer sip of champagne. He had been looking at their quivery reflections in the water. Now he looked at Pulovski.

"David's not cut out to be a cop, Mr. Pulovski. He's just not cut out for it . . ."

"I thought you were gonna be direct," Pulovski cut in.

Ackerman nodded. "So I was," he said.

He reached into the breast pocket of the designer suit and extracted two bills with an unfamiliar face—William McKinley—on them that Pulovski happened to know because of seizures they sometimes made. McKinley's was the face on a $500 bill.

Ackerman slipped them into the breast pocket of the sports jacket Pulovski was wearing.

"I just want to guarantee my son's safety," he said, smiling slightly.

Pulovski got a look on his face as if Ackerman had just slipped cat turds in his pocket. He pulled the cigar from his mouth and dropped it—it went hiss—into Ackerman's champagne glass.

"Mr. Ackerman, if you want a guarantee . . . buy a toaster."

He turned and walked away. A stunned Ackerman watched him go. If money didn't appeal to a man, what would? There weren't many things more powerful.

Pulovski went into the house and spotted David and Sarah dancing. For the moment David Ackerman was happy, lost in the love and joy of the beautiful Sarah.

Pulovski's voice cut the insulation away. "Hey, kid."

Ackerman turned and he and Sarah stopped dancing. Pulovski approached. In his hand was the $1000 Eugene Ackerman had given him.

"Next time," Pulovski said, "your old man wants a babysitter, tell him to try the Yellow Pages. It's cheaper."

He stuck the bills in Ackerman's jacket pocket. Then Pulovski left, and David Ackerman looked across the room at the figure of Eugene Ackerman, standing in the patio entrance. They stared, and David Ackerman felt the usual rage starting to boil up.

"Let's get the fuck out of here," he said. "Happy birthday."

Outside, David approached his Kawasaki 750 as if it had offended him greatly.

He straddled the bike, put the ignition key in, and turned.

It didn't start.

He tried again.

Dead.

Ackerman pounded the handlebars, then hopped off the

bike and kicked it, and it toppled over. Ackerman followed with some more kicks, destroying the mirrors and display console.

"I guess," Sarah said, "I should call us a cab."

Ackerman turned around. Sarah looked at him as concerned as much as she was bemused.

Ackerman nodded, then took the two $500 bills from his jacket pocket, crumpled them, and dropped them on the ground. Then he grabbed Sarah by the arm and they started walking away.

Pulovski had stood in the shadows twenty yards away and had watched them. When they were gone, he walked over to the bike, looked at it, then reached down and picked up the bills and stuffed them in his jacket pocket. What the fuck, he thought.

CHAPTER
15

MUCH of the modernistic house that Erich Strom used at the beach was glass, the better to view the ocean that it overlooked. Now, at night, the interior light spilled out onto the beach, illuminating a broad area around it.

Morales walked along the beach as he approached the house. The area was not exactly a teeming metropolis—the houses that flanked the house were a good seventy-five yards away, but Morales had stayed out of jail by learning to pay attention to details, and always acting with extreme caution. He made believe he was walking the surf.

Making noise would be no problem. The waves hissed and crashed, and his entire approach would be on sand. No one could hear him. He would be as quiet as a mouse.

And perhaps as nervous. Strom was unpredictable. The last Morales had heard Strom had gone to the airport, but you never knew. He was a snake. A vicious snake, and if

Morales got caught doing what he was about to do, he could be in trouble.

But he didn't have much choice. That fucking Pulovski had his *cojónes* in a vise. It was do this or tighten the vise. Morales was not a big man, and the only way he had avoided being made a punk on his one trip to the joint was because he had known an old Mafioso named Tony D. who put out the word that Morales was not to be touched.

But Tony had died, and now he had no one.

The best thing to do was to avoid prison.

Also, Pulovski said he realized Morales was taking a big risk. If he brought this off he would get him two large and wouldn't bother him for a long time.

Morales came within twenty-five yards of the reflected house light and stopped, then took a final look around and went up along the side of the house and circled it.

No cars were in the driveway, and there was no sign of life within. He decided it was safe to go in.

Getting in was simple. He had a key.

The beauty of it was that Strom would never know.

Inside, he waited in the darkened foyer and listened.

No sound.

He walked down the foyer, into a living room that had an expansive view of the ocean.

He went directly to the wine cabinet, took out a bottle and poured himself a glass, took a quick swig, then returned the wine bottle to the cabinet and placed the glass of wine on top of a marble table next to a leather couch. It was a safety net.

From his inside jacket pocket he extracted a low-frequency transmitter. It was a barrel-shaped device about a half inch wide and one inch long with an antenna as thin as a human hair.

Its range was about one hundred yards, but that's all Pulovski wanted. Plus it was less likely to cause interference on the TV like a high-frequency transmitter could.

Morales knew just where he was going to place it.

He got under the marble table and used two-faced tape to secure it on the underside of the table behind a leg. Then he used a dab of white glue to adhere the antenna to the marble.

That was it . . .

The sound made him go hollow in the belly. The front door was opening!

Morales knew the house. There was no fast way out from this end. He would have to gut it through.

He sat down on the leather couch and picked up the wineglass.

The door opened and closed and a moment later Strom, accompanied by Liesl, came into the room.

Strom stopped at the doorway. He did not speak for a moment.

"I see," Strom said, "you're as adept at breaking into houses as into cars."

Morales sipped the wine, smiled broadly, said lightly, "I like to keep sharp. You wanted to talk to me about something."

Strom would say what. Oh, a little misunderstanding Morales would then say . . .

Strom said nothing. He walked over to a chair that faced where Morales was and sat down. Liesl stayed near the doorway. Morales didn't like it.

"It's over, Morales," he said. "You're over."

Strom paused.

"*I don't have patience for any more shit.* That cop was learning too much too quick."

Strom paused again.

"You rely too much on nonexistent racial togetherness. A

few ounces of shit and your compatriot Little Felix was singing to me like Janet Jackson in heat.''

Morales shook his head. He knew he was in deep trouble. He tried to remain calm.

Strom's eyes had become gay. Morales had seen him like this. He was extremely dangerous.

''Between the cops and those fucking Italians I'm going to have to leave the country. You've caused me a lot of trouble.''

Morales knew that if he did not move he was dead. He bolted from the chair—he was very fast. But Liesl was in his way and just before he got to her she whirled around and delivered a karate kick to his jaw. He crashed heavily to the floor.

Strom stood above him, Liesl at his side. They were both smiling slightly. Morales was so scared he felt like throwing up.

CHAPTER
16

THE call came through on 911. It was from a crane operator in an auto graveyard on the outskirts of Los Angeles and it was particularly hysterical. Small wonder. While in the process of loading a blue BMW on top of a pile of cars the trunk had popped open—as often happened—and had spilled out the body of a dark-haired Hispanic man.

The call went into homicide and one of the detectives contacted Lieutenant Ray Garcia, who had initiated the homicide investigation into Erich Strom, a man who was intimately involved with chop shops.

When the detective, whose name was Bridges, described the man—a short Hispanic with deep-set eyes and prominent forehead—it sounded familiar. So Garcia, in turn, made another call to Nick Pulovski.

A half hour later Pulovski, Ackerman, and Garcia were threading their way through a crowd of onlookers, then cops and reporters, to the dump site.

It was apparent to Pulovski and Garcia, though not to the inexperienced Ackerman, that the dead man had been worked over by experts before he had been done; the fall couldn't do what was done to him. Plus he had the old wiseguy way of identifying a pigeon; they had cut his cock off.

Garcia had called Nick because he thought he might be able to make the body.

"It sounded like the canary you had inside Strom's operation."

Now Pulovski looked and slowly shook his head.

"Not Morales. Absolutely not. That ain't him."

Ackerman glanced sharply at Pulovski. It absolutely was Morales, but he said nothing. They left and as they did Pulovski thought that yes it absolutely was Morales, but he was not about to serve some of it up to the homicide dicks on a platter. This was his case—and he was taking it to the finish.

CHAPTER
17

A FTER learning of Morales's death, Pulovski immediately went out to Strom's house with Ackerman and
set up shop. He used a special receiver to see if he
could pick up any transmittance.

With great joy, he discovered that Morales had succeeded.

"We'll be able to hear if someone farts in that room,"
Pulovski said to Ackerman, who he had told about the bug.
"This thing can pick up whispers at twenty feet. Morales did
good."

Ackerman nodded, but he was just a little appalled by
Pulovski's attitude about Morales's death—he couldn't care
less. But Morales was human, Ackerman might say. He could
almost hear Pulovski's response to that: "Bullshit. He was
just an asshole."

After picking up the signal, Pulovski set up a receiver—
basically a stereo radio—and he and Ackerman started to
wait to see what, if anything, someone would say that could

help in the investigation of Strom. Ackerman had decided that that was all Pulovski and he were going to do until the case was cleared.

Now, just dawn, Pulovski was in the back of the car, Ackerman the front. Pulovski had a jack wire in his ear and was listening. They had been there ten hours and the back, Ackerman noted, was beginning to look like Pulovski's apartment.

Pulovski had brought some paper cups for the huge thermos of coffee they had, and the cups and wrappers were strewn over the place. He had put one cigar out on the floor of the car.

They had worked their way through one box of donuts and there was another on the dash jammed under the rear window.

Plus the car, despite the fact that Ackerman had all the windows open, smelled. Smelled of Pulovski's cigars, of the cheap Scotch he drank, and just the natural effects of men in close quarters who haven't bathed in a while.

All night, too, Ackerman had been disturbed by what they were doing. It was wrong. Dead wrong. And he was only on the job two years. If they got caught, he could lose his job.

But he had not said anything to Pulovski, despite his worries. It would only lead to more criticism. Still, as he sat there and the light came up, the sheer reality of what they were doing started to get to him. He swallowed.

"We could really get in a lot of trouble for this," Ackerman said.

Pulovski had just taken a swig of the whiskey and eyed him with a certain glint in his eyes.

"Relax, kid, take your mind off my work. Think about that squeeze at your daddy's little bash the other night . . ."

Ackerman felt a hot surge of anger. "Just *shut up* about her."

Pulovski was distracted by static on the radio, which had not been working well. He adjusted the reception, slapped it a little. It was working again.

"Why didn't we file a warrant?"

Pulovski looked at him foully. "Well, first off," he said, his voice tinged with scorn, "he would turn us down. It ain't our case, remember?"

"Then why are we here?"

Pulovski said nothing.

"We both recognized Morales—why'd you lie to Garcia?"

"I didn't lie to him," Pulovski said, "I just didn't tell the truth."

"Goddamn it, don't patronize me! You think I like dragging around after you? I fucking hate it!"

Pulovski acted as if Ackerman hadn't said a thing, and then turned his head a bit so Ackerman could see the other side of it. He had a finger in his ear, and his expression said: can't hear you.

Ackerman leaned over the back of the car. Ackerman yelled in his face. "And I hate the way you drive! And I hate your stinking whiskey breath. And I . . ."

Pulovski suddenly cut in.

". . . and I hate your uptight regulation-spouting Boy Scout horseshit, kid! And I hate those obnoxious creases in your pants. And I . . ."

Pulovski reached back and grabbed the box of donuts and threw them out the window, one by one . . .

". . . I hate," Pulovski said, "your fucking fruitcake donuts with those goddamn sprinkles and pink shit all over them!"

"Well, then maybe you should . . ."

But Pulovski had taken his finger and plugged his open ear again and Ackerman reached over and pulled the earpiece out of Pulovski's ear and Pulovski responded by throwing a hard punch . . .

. . . and was shocked when the kid grabbed it in mid-arc and held it rigid while Pulovski pushed forward and Ackerman back . . . and Pulovski's fist went nowhere . . . and their eyes were locked in loathing . . .

And then Pulovski relaxed, and Ackerman let go, and Pulovski put the earpiece back in his ear.

They were silent for a moment. It was a clash that had bled off some of the tension in their relationship and sitting in a car ten hours waiting for something to happen . . .

"Why," Ackerman said, "do you want this guy so badly?"

"He did my partner."

"I know . . . but I sense something else . . ."

Pulovski said nothing. He took out his flask and took a long drink. He had not denied what the kid said. Now he confirmed it.

"All my life," he said, "I've been in the race . . . on the circuit . . . and I've only come up small-time . . . Then this guy Strom fell into my lap. Sheer luck. Me and Parker realized we're onto the biggest chop shop operation of our life where we had a shot at doing something . . ."

He paused, then continued, "I'm wearing this son of a bitch down, kid . . . he's running on reserve, his engine's gonna blow . . ."

He took another swig, his eyes filled with fire . . .

"And goddamn, but I'm gonna win this one. And you can either stay out of my way, kid, or you can be my partner and back me up."

Ackerman was still. He said nothing. Pulovski started to peel the cellophane off a fresh cigar . . .

Ackerman was grateful that at least now he understood what Pulovski was doing—and why. He was investigating Strom but, maybe more important, he was harassing him until he cracked and made a mistake. And, at the same time Ackerman knew, Pulovski was getting great pleasure out of breaking his balls.

But there was one thing Pulovski said that made Ackerman feel queasy: ". . . or you can be my partner and back me up."

Like everything else in his life, Ackerman wondered just how good a backup he could be.

He just hoped to hell that, at least for now, he wouldn't have to find out.

Ackerman was aware that he was very tired—and was being shook awake. He opened his eyes.

Pulovski was holding a second earphone toward him.

"Listen. All things come to them who wait."

He listened, and his eyes widened and he was suddenly wide awake.

"Kid," Pulovski said, "we just hit the jackpot. Let's get the fuck on the road."

CHAPTER
18

THE Four Aces Casino, located in West Los Angeles, was immense, as well it might be, it being the only place in the city where legal gambling—only cards—was allowed.

The place was the size of a cattle barn and looked like it had been transplanted from downtown Las Vegas. The facade was pure glitz and its name, Four Aces, was written across it in three-foot-high letters formed of neon playing cards. Demure it wasn't.

Inside, the casino was just as glitzy—and super busy. It was filled with gaming tables, gamblers sitting around intently playing every game known to man, including a Chinese card game pai gow. It was a frenetic place, but controlled.

The games were played with chips, but the gamblers were watched very closely.

There was a raised podium on which was a big, beefy, dark-haired man named Alphonse, the floor manager who oversaw everything. With the kind of money—millions—

that changed hands here there was always the implicit threat of corruption, or plain stealing.

Of course those in the know would be reluctant to steal, because the casino was owned by the Mafia, and they had their own superb police force and judicial system.

At least two thieves had been apprehended, tried, and sentenced by the wiseguys and both had been found in dumpsters in similar shape. They had been "jointed"—cut up into a number of pieces but their heads had been left intact and each had a sign on the forehead saying "Thief" that had been secured with a sixteen-penny gutter spike. Only addicts or similarly desperate folk would test this system.

Shortly after noon, Strom and Liesl entered the Four Aces Casino. Unlike 99.9 percent of the people in the place, they were more interested in other people—such as the three dead-eyed gorillas who were obvious enforcers—than the cards or the chips on the table. They headed toward one of the tables. They both knew that very shortly all hell was going to break loose.

One flight down, in the men's bathroom, Angelo Cruz, the member of Strom's crew who favored the stiletto, was sitting on one of the toilets, fully dressed. He checked his watch. It was time.

He put the parcel he had carried in out of sight directly behind the bowl and stepped out of the stall. The bathroom was empty. He exited the room quickly.

Upstairs, Loco Martinez sat at a table in a restaurant off the main room finishing a meal. He checked his watch, wiped his mouth, dropped some money on the table, and made his way slowly out of the casino. Unnoticed by anyone was a bag he left under the table.

Twenty seconds after Loco left, the smoke bomb that Cruz had placed behind the toilet went off, the explosion muffled but terrifying, sending one man who had been on an adjacent bowl scuttling out of the bathroom with his pants at his knees.

The bathroom quickly filled up with black smoke, and seeped into the hall—and activated and set the alarm system off.

The gamblers upstairs hardly had time to react when the smoke bomb that Loco had planted under the table went off, and within seconds the upstairs alarms were clanging with an earsplitting intensity and intermingled with the screams and people yelling "FIRE!" and running to the exits, rushing to save their lives.

The restaurant filled with smoke and billowed into the casino proper. Very soon it was pure chaos.

Smoke had blocked the vision of the floor manager, Alphonse, who came down from the podium and was frantically looking for his assistants to help him create some kind of order. He knew the bombs weren't explosive.

He could not see them but then he heard the calm voice to his right and an arm was placed over his shoulder—and he looked down to see an automatic pressed into his ribs.

"Keep walking," Strom said, "or I'll give you a permanent bellyache."

No one noticed as Alphonse, flanked by Strom and Liesl, who had slipped up on the other side, walked through the chaos toward the stairs door that led downstairs.

Outside, people and smoke poured out the doors and no one noticed when a blue van with black-tinted windows drove up slowly and parked opposite the main entrance. Loco was driving.

Inside, Liesl and Strom opened the door to the dimly lit stairwell. The door closed behind them and Strom immediately rammed Alphonse against the wall and stuck his H & K automatic in his mouth. Cruz, who had joined the others in the stairwell, slipped a crowbar through the door handles, barring entry.

"I know you dumb guinees launder money here," Strom said. "So you've got clean money and dirty money in the vault, and I happen to know that at any given moment you got two million in it. Luckily, I don't care if the money is clean or dirty. I'll take it all, and you're going to take us to it, Alphonse, or I'm going to pull the trigger and redecorate this wall. Is that clear?"

Alphonse blinked yes and both Strom and Liesl smiled. This was fun.

Thirty seconds later Strom, Liesl, Cruz, and Alphonse were standing in a room that was empty except for stacks of crates piled up against one wall.

Cruz proceeded to push them out of the way, and gradually a massive vault as high as a regular door appeared.

Strom pushed Alphonse toward the vault.

"Do it," Strom said.

Alphonse nodded and placed sweaty fingers on the lock and started to turn, occasionally blinking to clear the sweat from his eyes.

Then it was finished and Alphonse started to open the door but Strom pushed him aside and opened the door and was just about to step inside when his mouth dropped and he simultaneously was smacked in the head with the butt of a gun.

The blow sent Strom to the ground, his gun clattering across the floor.

Pulovski, unlit cigar jammed into his mouth, stepped out. He leveled his Beretta at Liesl and Cruz.

"Freeze, assholes. Up against the fucking wall! *Do it!*"

They did it.

Pulovski dragged Strom to his feet and pushed him toward them.

Outside, Loco was getting impatient, watching the door, knowing that they should be out very soon . . .

Then he heard sirens wailing.

He didn't know what to do, and then the decision was made for him.

Two black and whites screeched into the street one way, followed by another . . . and another . . .

Cops poured out drawing guns as they ran toward the door to the casino. Among the cops, though Loco didn't know him, was a plainclothes cop—Lieutenant Ray Garcia.

Putana, Loco said, then pulled the van away.

Downstairs, Pulovski still had his piece leveled at Liesl and Cruz.

It had worked out perfectly. Pulovski had called Alphonse and had agreed to give him a very important tip—based on one condition: Pulovski be allowed to run the show his way.

Alphonse had no choice, and Pulovski told him: He was going to be heisted, to get the money out of the vault. Pulovski would wait inside and take care of everything.

Then Alphonse had tried to renege, telling Pulovski he would get "his own people."

Pulovski had been direct: "If you do that I'll be on you," he had said, "like stink on shit for the rest of your natural life."

Alphonse had let him run it his way.

Pulovski smiled. For the rest of *his* life he would carry the stunned look Strom got on his face when he walked out of the vault. It was one of—what was the word—chagrin. Shock and chagrin. Total fucking chagrin.

"You bastard," Strom said, "how did you know?"

"That's just what life is like when you've got a bug up your ass, scumbag."

Pulovski turned to Alphonse, who was toweling off his face. "You did good, Alphonse. Take a hike."

Alphonse was glad to leave, and as he left David Ackerman came in. Here, Pulovski thought, comes the cavalry. Actually, Pulovski had told the kid to call in an "Officer needs assistance" to Garcia as soon as he spotted Strom.

"Cover them good, partner," Pulovski said to the kid.

Pulovski headed toward Strom, preparatory to patting him and the others down, something he figured he would really enjoy with the squeeze. Maybe a finger would linger a little here and there . . .

Liesl looked over her shoulder—at Ackerman.

His gun was out, but he was shaky. His face twitched. He was aware that he was now the backup.

Liesl turned from the wall and headed toward Ackerman.

"Oh, thank God . . . they dragged me down here."

Pulovski, busy with Strom, glanced up sharply. "Shoot her, kid! Shoot her!"

Ackerman didn't know what to do. He . . .

"Stop!" he said. "Stop. Please, miss, I . . ."

"Shit," Pulovski yelled and turned to shoot Liesl and was kicked in the stomach by Strom.

Ackerman turned his gun to Strom but out of the side of his eye saw a lightning movement and heard a single word from Liesl: "*Amateur*."

And then his gun was kicked out of his hand, and she drove her elbow into his solar plexus and Ackerman was down. Strom had scooped up Pulovski's gun and then ripped out the .22 in the ankle holster.

Ackerman looked at his gun, and made a desperate lunge for it . . .

Strom shot him twice in the back.

He flopped on the floor, dead still.

Strom turned the piece toward Pulovski, moaning, half unconscious.

He wanted him to be a little more alert to know what was coming . . .

"Erich!"

Strom turned toward the vault that Liesl had gone into.

"There's nothing in here. Nothing!"

Strom was speechless. He understood what had happened.

"What are we going to do?" Liesl said.

Strom, whose finger had tightened on the trigger, lowered the gun. He smiled a smile reserved for when he was truly enjoying something.

"We're going to improvise," he said.

CHAPTER
19

RAY Garcia was pissed. As he approached the Four Aces Casino—which was pure chaos—he could bet what Pulovski had done: timed the call to alert Garcia about the heist just a bit late—so the son of a bitch could do it all himself—or with himself and the new kid.

The main gambling room was almost empty when he went inside, followed by a stream of cops, guns at the ready.

Nick was nowhere in sight, and neither was the kid. All the kid had said was that Nick said to come quick—there's a heist going down.

But where? This floor. Was there another floor . . . ?

He was wondering what to do next when he saw something that made him go hollow. He yelled to the phalanx of cops behind him.

"Hold your fire! Don't shoot. Jesus, Nick . . . Jesus . . ."

Erich Strom was coming out of the stairwell and he had Nick in a choke hold, an automatic in his mouth. What must be the girlfriend Nick briefed him on was next to him, and there was another punk with him.

Strom's eyes looked strange.

"There's already one dead cop downstairs. *Don't make it two*."

Garcia sensed a terrible moment when he thought some of the cops were going to fire. Nick would die . . .

But they didn't.

Strom spoke again: "If you want him to die, shoot now. If not, listen to me. We're going to walk to the parking lot outside."

Garcia shook his head. "We can't let you out of here. You know that."

Strom smiled. "Fine," he said, "in five seconds, I'm pulling the trigger. Five . . . four . . . three . . . two . . ."

"All right!" Garcia shouted to Strom. "Hold your fire . . . let them out of the building."

Strom pushed Pulovski forward, followed by Liesl and the punk. The cops' guns followed them, as if they were magnetized, and then the cops parted slowly, very reluctantly, as they went through.

They went into the parking lot adjacent to the building. It was filled with black and whites—red bubble gum lights still going—and ten to fifteen cops, guns drawn.

Strom moved slowly, carefully, gun still in Pulovski's mouth. And the cops' guns followed him and the others.

Garcia had followed them outside.

"Listen to me," Strom said, "this pig has just cheated me out of two million dollars in cash. And that's exactly what you'll have for me in twenty-four hours if you ever want to see him alive again."

The blood drained from Garcia's face.

"*Two million bucks?* Are you out of your fucking mind?"

"That's not pertinent, is it?" Strom said, stepping over to

a black and white. "We are taking this car out of here. I'm going to be flipping through all your frequencies for the next hour, and if I hear one static peep following us, the pig dies."

Pulovski tried to say no with his eyes.

By the book, Garcia should say no—he couldn't allow Strom to do this.

By the book, Nick Pulovski would die.

"We hear you," Garcia said. "How can we be sure you won't kill him anyway?"

"You can't, can you?"

Garcia and the other cops watched impotently as Cruz jumped behind the driver's seat and Strom got in the front, forcing Pulovski in with him. Liesl got in the back.

A moment later the car was screeching out of the lot.

"Nick," Garcia said in pain and anger, "goddamn it all to hell."

Then from the side of his eye a distraction: coming out the door . . .

David Ackerman. He stripped off his shirt, and beneath it was the soft body armor. From far away his body was alive. From close up his eyes were dead . . .

CHAPTER
20

SOMEONE once said that police headquarters, a big, gray building festooned with gingerbread and big windows that never seemed to be clean, was a "monument of an architect to a mother he loathed."

But that wasn't true. It had been a beautiful building when it was erected in the late 1920s, but time had passed it by. It was old, gray, perhaps a little anachronistic as a unit in a modern police force.

Nick Pulovski had always had warm feelings for the building but not, as he would say, "its contents. Brass assholes who park their keisters all day and only come to scenes to get their faces in the paper."

Now, David Ackerman was sitting at a table in the operations room on the tenth floor, an untouched cup of coffee on the table in front of him.

Around him, the cops went about their business, but Ackerman did not feel part of any of it. He felt outside, alone, as alone as he used to feel in the long afternoons in his parents' house when he played alone in his room and waited for them to return from one trip or another.

And, now he knew, the old feeling was emerging. One, in a sense, that he always knew he had had a preordained rendezvous with. A rendezvous with his true self, what a psychiatrist he had seen once called his "persona in shadow." A persona that, he knew, was nothing, as typified by his reactions at the Four Aces Casino that afternoon.

The circle was complete. He had fought it, but it was destiny. You could not change destiny.

Nor could he live with it.

It was unbearable for him to think of Nick, and every time an image of his face flashed into consciousness, Ackerman thought it away. The image of what Strom could be doing to him would follow, and that would be excruciating, totally unacceptable.

Now, he waited for Lieutenant Garcia to come out of a meeting with Captain Bill Hargate, an important member of the brass. He was waiting to learn what they were going to do about Strom's ransom demand—and what was going to happen to him.

Garcia had gone into Hargate's office only two minutes earlier, so Ackerman was surprised when he came out with Hargate, an imposing-looking black man. They were talking as they approached Ackerman, and though he couldn't hear any of it he could imagine it by what Garcia's body language said. Garcia looked angry, depressed.

And he was.

"What do you mean, no money?"

"I mean the PC and the mayor have decided not to set a precedent that would invite every maniac in this city to kidnap somebody. Whatever the hell we do, we're going to have to do it without two million dollars."

"They'll kill him, goddamn it!"

"*Then they'll kill him*," Hargate snapped, and then said

something that cut deep into Garcia. "You should never have let them out of there."

Garcia spoke softly, close to tears. "He was going to squeeze that trigger. I could see it in his eyes."

Whalen, an overweight, old-time cop known on the job as a "hairbag"—a not unaffectionate term—walked over to Garcia and Hargate.

He spoke to Hargate. "They found the car ditched in East LA," he said. "Of course the perps were long gone."

Hargate nodded and a moment later they were standing near Ackerman. Hargate looked at him, total disdain in his eyes.

"You took it in the back, didn't you?"

Ackerman didn't look up. He couldn't. He could not look into the eyes of another cop.

Hargate snorted in disgust and left. Garcia stayed behind. He looked at Ackerman who, again, did not look up.

"Take a vacation. Whatever happens, I don't want to see your face for at least two weeks."

Ackerman got up and, like a zombie, walked out of the room.

CHAPTER
21

IT was late when David Ackerman returned to his house. He did not know how late. He wasn't noticing things outside himself. His mind was turned inward, relentlessly inward.

Sarah was there, waiting anxiously for him. Accounts of what had happened at the Four Aces Casino were all over the tube and she had come over immediately.

She was extremely concerned and wanted very much to make love to David, but he said he wasn't in the mood right now. He strove with all his might to hide the things rumbling inside him.

He could not bear to tell her that he didn't feel worthy enough for her love.

Then they finished talking—saying nothing—and lay down in bed together and when Ackerman heard her even breathing he knew she was asleep.

He got up and went over to the window and sat down and looked out.

There was not much to see if he could see. Just homes across the street, streetlights, parked cars, and his own handsome image palely reflected in the glass.

Nothing.

Now, he tried to stop the images from returning, but he knew he couldn't. This time he could not. They were too strong.

The secret. The terrible secret came back to him. The incident. The one that forever and ever and ever defined him.

He closed his eyes.

It was him, and his older brother Eugene, Jr. Gene and Davey. That's what his mother and father always called them. Gene and Davey.

They were on a roof, just young kids, playing cops and robbers. It was such a happy time, such a wonderful time.

A hand reached up inside Ackerman and squeezed his insides tightly. His fists clenched.

The cap pistols exploded and the cop, Gene, pursued the bad guy, Davey, across the roof.

Davey hid behind a water tower, and they exchanged fire, but Davey knew he had to get away. He would get away. He was daring. Always daring.

There was one way he might get away, because even though Gene was older he was not as athletic as Davey. He could not do the things Davey could do . . .

So Davey left the shelter of the water tower and ran toward the edge of the roof and built up speed and leapt off, soaring through the air, and beneath him five stories down, an alley, but he made it easily . . .

And he ran and took shelter and then he turned and looked and Gene was in midair above the alley and Davey knew he wasn't going to make it and he didn't quite . . . he hit the ledge of the roof and then slid back and held on and called for Davey who was frozen and scared . . .

"Help me! . . . Help me!"

And then the scene changed, and Davey got a quick savage image. The woman coming toward him and he could see Nick's contorted face . . .

"Shoot her! Shoot her!"

. . . and then he was back on the roof and he couldn't move, and then he could and he went down the stairs running to get help for Gene because he was too scared to help himself . . .

. . . and Strom's bullets slammed into his back, and Nick was gone . . . and so was Gene.

Tears streamed down Ackerman's face. He sobbed softly, deeply, the regret bottomless, the realization of what he had done unbearable. He wished that he had not had the body armor on . . .

A thought. He could eat his Beretta. No. He could not do that to Sarah. Don't do that to her.

How considerate he was! What a good guy!

Mechanically he rose and started to walk across the bedroom. He glanced across at Sarah, still asleep . . .

Another image: the day of the funeral, his father and mother in black; and he in a little boy's dark suit and his father had looked across at him and he said nothing but his eyes said it all: Your cowardice has taken my son from me, something that will never come again . . .

And it was a look, he thought, that he had seen ever since that day. It had never really left his father's eyes, and always stood like a barrier between them, a barrier that never could be crossed.

The hand in his stomach squeezed harder.

Pulovski. Maybe he saw what it was. Maybe that is why he treated me so badly.

He knew that when it was on the line I would leave him hanging off the edge of a building.

Now, Ackerman stood in front of the bathroom mirror and

looked at himself. A handsome face, the eyes red with tears, the face of nothing.

Something screamed inside and he gripped the edges of the lavatory and pounded his head into the cabinet mirror, shattering it, blood spraying on the glass.

He went over and grabbed a towel and covered his face with it.

Something shifted inside him. He was at ground zero.

In just that moment, he realized that something profound had happened inside him.

He was very dangerous because he realized that he did not care if he lived or died.

The sound awakened Sarah. Ten seconds later she was in the living room.

"David!" He was nowhere to be seen.

And then he came out of the bathroom and her stomach lurched.

His hair was slicked back, blood had run down his face creating a kind of red scar—and in one hand was his holster, in the other his Beretta.

"David," Sarah said, her voice suffused with concern, "what happened to you?"

Ackerman said nothing. He walked over to a table and pulled out a drawer and extracted three magazine cartridges. He jammed two in his pocket and one into the gun. Then he put the gun in the shoulder holster and strapped it on.

Sarah walked up to him as he adjusted the holster. "What's going on, David," she said, looking at the rivulet of dried blood on his face.

He looked at her. There was something in his eyes that scared her.

"It's time," he said, "for me to stop being afraid."

"I don't think I like this."

His eyes went flat.

"Nobody asked you to."

Suddenly there was a void between them, a void, she sensed, that she could not cross.

She watched him pick up his motorcycle helmet and jacket and go out the door without saying good-bye.

She went into the bathroom. There was glass all over the place, some of the shards spotted with blood. She picked up a piece and looked at it. She was very, very afraid.

CHAPTER
22

THE plane, a Falcon 20 cargo jet, was on one of the far runways of Los Angeles International Airport, far away from the busier areas that handled passenger traffic. Planes in this area were mostly the cargo type.

The twin-engine plane, all white with a blue stripe down the side, stood near an aluminum hangar, where it had been parked for some time, just being removed the night before by Blackwell, the crusty Texas pilot.

Now the door opened and the steps fed out of the plane hydraulically until on the ground. Blackwell emerged. He looked annoyed—and he was.

Strom, he thought, should be at the warehouse—unless the wiseguys got to him. But he doubted that very much. Blackwell knew wiseguys didn't move that quick. Anyway, the warehouse was a location that only a few people had known about.

But he could be anywhere, because Blackwell knew he used a cellular phone—the phone was there . . . the place didn't matter.

Still, he should have been at the airport—or called.

Blackwell called from a pay phone near the hangar.

"Yes," Strom said.

"What the hell is going on?" Blackwell said. "You were supposed to be here five hours ago."

"Complications, Blackwell," Erich Strom said. "Life's full of them. I'm going to need you there at exactly the same time, tomorrow night."

Blackwell wasn't buying explanations.

"What do you think this is, nothing? I called in a lot of IOUs for this. I'll try and swing it, but it'll probably cost a lot more. And if you can't make it, call."

"Just make sure you're there," Strom said.

Strom *was* speaking from the warehouse—three floors above the repair shop where Pulovski and Ackerman had dropped in for a visit with Max and had spotted Loco's gruesome green car that was in exactly the same spot—in the area with the TV monitors.

Arrayed around the floor were cars in various states of cannibalization, except two—a black and a white Mercedes.

Nick Pulovski was also there, sitting in a chair with his hands bound behind him and his feet bound to the chair. Next to him was a stainless steel and metal table.

Strom looked at Pulovski. Something occurred to him. He approached Pulovski. Liesl walked along with him.

"Well, cop," he said, "you wanted me so badly. Now you're getting to spend the last few hours of your life with me."

"Makes me go all warm inside, scumbag."

Strom smiled. "You know, I'm just dying of curiosity. Out of all the scumbags in the world—why me?"

"You just happened to be in my line of fire . . . and one scumbag is as good as the next . . ."

Pulovski paused.

". . . scumbag," he finished.

Abruptly Liesl whacked him sharply across the face. She glared at him. He smiled.

"You can do better'n that, darlin' . . . you didn't even hurt my pride."

Fluidly, with power fueled by a controlled rage, Liesl smashed Pulovski in the head so hard it snapped back and he and the chair toppled over. He just missed smacking his head on the concrete.

Strom shook his head and pulled Pulovski upright again.

"Liesl, that's no way to treat two million dollars' worth of merchandise, is it?"

He smiled at Pulovski, who spit blood.

Then, all were distracted by the appearance of Max, who had been working on something behind the video monitors. It soon became apparent what it was when he handed Strom a small rectangular control device about the size of a walkie-talkie.

"Place is all rigged, Mr. Strom," he said. "Just dial the sequence anywhere from within two hundred yards of this place and"—he smiled—"boom!—they'll have to redraw the maps to the area!"

Pulovski looked at Max. His eyes said: You failed me, kid, and you fucked up.

Max stared at him.

"Looks like I wasn't the one who needed longer legs, hey, Pulovski?"

Strom approached Pulovski. His eyes glittered with that peculiar two quarts low quality. He smiled. He leaned close to Pulovski.

"I'm going to have to leave this place real soon thanks to you. But when I go . . . I go with a bang! So do you."

Pulovski's eyes said what they said a lot of the time: Asshole.

CHAPTER
23

PULOVSKI'S house and the yard behind it were unlit, the only light a pale light that spilled from adjacent buildings. Everything was the same as it had been when David Ackerman had first visited him there after being beaten up at La Casa Blanca . . . the cannibalized cars, the tools strewn over the yard, and, hulking in the middle of it all, the Harley Sportster under the tarp.

David Ackerman entered the yard. He was dressed in dungarees and leather jacket and the blood was still on his face.

He went immediately to the same brick where the key to the Harley had been located and picked it up. Then he went to the Harley and carefully removed the tarp and placed it on the ground.

Even in the dim light the machine glittered and even stationary it exuded power. It was, indeed, a classic.

Ackerman climbed on and slipped the key in the ignition and turned. It hammered to life. He switched on the lights and a minute later maneuvered the bike out of the yard. Inside, he had never felt closer to a machine. It was as if it were flesh and blood; as if he were riding an old and powerful living ally, an animal and not a machine.

La Casa Blanca looked—and sounded—the same to Ackerman as it did when he and Pulovski first went there. Such places never change much—the decorators don't visit that frequently—except they regularly go out of business.

Ackerman pulled the old Harley to within thirty yards of the bar and dismounted. He pulled his helmet off, hooked it to the back of the bike, then started walking toward the bar.

Inside, two forces pulled at him: rage and fear.

He was terribly, ferociously angry, yet beneath the fire was his old friend—or enemy—fear. The question was which one would win.

He got halfway to the bar and stopped. He turned and started walking back to the bike.

And stopped again. He knew that if he couldn't go into that bar now he would forever leave the Gene Ackermans and the Nick Pulovskis out there, waiting to die. And, too, he would be over himself, the living dead.

Something roared and broke inside him. He turned and started walking back to the bar—and entered.

All eyes, seemingly, were immediately on him and recognized him as the pussy cop that had been in earlier. Now, a few noticed that he looked two quarts low. His eyes were glazed, the blood from his head's collision with the mirror dried into a kind of fearsome scar.

He walked to the bar and pushed between two Chicano bikers.

The big, bearded bartender, cigar clamped in rancid teeth, came up and blew a cloud of smoke in Ackerman's face. It had no apparent effect.

"I'm looking for Loco Martinez."

The bartender let out with a belly laugh, then removed the cigar and spit in Ackerman's face. Ackerman stood there.

"Why don't you run home before you get hurt worse then before, sonny boy?"

Ackerman responded by grabbing the bartender's beard and pulling him forward. Then he removed the cigar and mashed the lit end in his face.

The bartender howled with agony—and the fight commenced.

From behind Ackerman a biker looped an arm around his neck and whirled him around, holding him fast, as another biker threw a hard punch into Ackerman's stomach and was about to do it again when Ackerman brought his foot up in a short, savage arc that connected perfectly with the biker's drooping scrotum and dropped him like a sack of potatoes.

Ackerman then entwined a leg between the legs of the biker with the choke hold and pushed back. The biker tripped and both men went crashing into a table, sending people scurrying, and an instant later Ackerman had grabbed a big lit candle jar and splashed the scalding wax in the eyes of his assailant, and then brought the jar around and knocked him senseless.

Inside Ackerman felt himself just starting to cook. He wanted more. He got them.

He was engulfed by bikers: one tackled him and knocked him down and then others were on top, pounding him . . .

And then someone shrieked: "Mato! Mato!!"

And the bikers on Ackerman, like a film reversing, were off him and the reason became apparent.

A man held two pit bull terriers, a gray and a roan one, by the collars. Their massive jaws were slavering, their Oriental eyes fixed on Ackerman, scraping the ground, trying to get at him.

He felt a twinge of fear, and then more. The man let the

dogs go and within a millisecond they were in full stride, heading straight at him.

He had one choice.

He ripped his Beretta from his shoulder holster and dropped into a modified Weaver stance just as the gray pit bull became airborne, heading for his neck.

Ackerman squeezed off a single shot; the bullet stalled the dog in midflight and buzzed through its heart; by the time it hit the bar floor it was dead meat.

The other dog had, meanwhile, clamped its unbelievably powerful jaws on one of Ackerman's boots. Ackerman could easily have shot it but he felt just as vicious as the dog and reached down and grabbed it by a leg, and with one hand ripped it savagely upward and tossed it over his head. It cartwheeled through the air and came down on a table, half collapsing it, and was knocked senseless.

He put his gun back in his holster. His heart was hammering, his eyes blazing. Something primitive and raw had been released, the rage of a lifetime.

"Anybody else? Come on, you fuckers. I'm here . . . Come on!"

Now he could see and smell the fear in the crowd, and the eyes that he met dropped to the floor.

He walked toward the bar, and as he did he pulled out the Beretta again.

The crowd reaction was instantaneous. They scurried to get out of the line of fire.

Then he stopped a few yards from the bar, and methodically started to blast the bottles off the back shelves one by one, like ducks in a gallery. Behind him, people were scurrying for the exit.

Then he grabbed a bottle of rum off the bar, smacked its top off, spilled it all over on the bar, picked a lighter up, and lit it. It burst into flame and he threw the bottle and what was left into the flame, making it billow furiously.

More people screamed and scurried for the exits. It was a total madhouse.

The bartender headed for the exit but Ackerman wasn't allowing that.

He reached over the counter and grabbed him by the shirt.

"You can't do this . . ." the bartender wailed. *"You're a cop, man, you're a fucking cop* . . ."

Ackerman held the Beretta just below his nose. "Oh, yeah? I'll tell you what I'll do. You're gonna tell me where I can find Loco or I'm *gonna blow your fucking kneecaps off and leave you here to burn."*

The bartender watched the gun. "I don't know where Loco runs . . . I swear on the Virgin . . . *nobody knows* . . ."

"How about Little Felix?"

The bartender was happy. He could tell Ackerman something he wanted to hear.

"Third and Howard . . . he runs the cleaners on Third and Howard."

Ackerman looked indecisive for a moment, then lowered the gun and reached into a jacket pocket and extracted two dollar bills. He put them on the bar.

"I never did pay for the beer," he said, and turned and exited. La Casa Blanca was finally being purified—by fire.

CHAPTER
24

THE air in the conference room at headquarters that had been set up as a command post was more dead than rank, but certainly not fresh. It was a blend of dead air and incipient body odor with a soupçon of bad breath and methane.

Dawn had arrived.

On the conference table were many empty coffee cups and the plates and containers of the food the men had eaten from.

There were five men in the room. Captain Hargate, Ray Garcia, a police public relations man, a man from the mayor's office, and Fred Davis, an FBI agent.

There was one phone and it was near Captain Hargate, who was in command. If and when Strom called, he would take it, though given the decision of the PC and the mayor —on advice from Hargate—it hardly seemed worthwhile. They were not going to pay the money. The die was cast.

Still, where there was life—and it was assumed Nick was still alive—there was hope . . . plus a phone trap. On the

PC's orders, all of Los Angeles had been "trapped," meaning that any call coming into the room from anywhere in Los Angeles and its environs could be traced rather rapidly . . . all of three minutes. Strom certainly sounded like a streetwise guy and would probably not talk long enough to be caught.

But there again, where there was life, there was hope.

The men—bedraggled, sweaty, and unshaven—except for Hargate who had taken a portable razor with him—had been in the room for twelve hours, and while all were tired, each knew that one thing would get the adrenaline pumping and surging: a call from Strom.

Most cops spent their careers changing from ordinary human beings into otherworldly creatures with skins like rhinos and fail-safe emotional systems that could filter out all but the most horrendous assaults on the spirit.

But two kinds of assaults would always reach any cop no matter how long he had been on the job, how many felony arrests he had made, how many dreams he had seen die, and how thick a skin he had developed.

One was the death of a child—any child. Many a cop had come on a scene where a child was dead and had cried and other cops, who would not find this acceptable macho behavior ordinarily, would understand and no one would say anything.

The other thing that got to cops was the death of another cop. Cops could no more not react to that than they could not react to eating dogshit.

For Ray Garcia, Nick Pulovski was even more than just any cop. He would never tell him, but to Garcia he was special. He was a pigheaded, cynical, semi-alcoholic, cigar-smoking, down-at-the-heels pain in the ass, but Garcia had always secretly admired his spirit. Once, when Garcia's wife was cutting some meat, he saw something that reminded him of that spirit in the meat: gristle. Tough, hard to chew, and you couldn't swallow it real well.

Pulovski was from the old school, a warrior, a cop's cop

that nothing in life could take down. He had suffered much in his career and his personal life, but there he was, always getting up off the deck, that unlit cigar in his mouth, undefeated. A piece of gristle . . .

Garcia blinked. Maybe he did do the wrong thing, maybe . . .

He stopped. Working himself over wouldn't serve any purpose.

He looked at the phone.

"C'mon," he said to himself, "ring. *Please*."

It rang, and suddenly the room was charged with electricity, adrenaline pumping.

Captain Hargate picked up after the first ring. His eyes said it all. It was Strom. Hargate put it on the speaker.

"I suppose," Strom said, "half the force is listening to our little conversation at this moment. Very well. I want the two million in cash, I don't care in what denominations or where you get it, in a single black suitcase. The dropoff spot will be Third and Kennedy at nine P.M. tonight. A man will come in a van and pick it up. You will follow him and receive further instructions as you go."

"Wait a minute. Pulovski's got to be at the drop," Hargate said.

"So that your sharpshooters can take my man out and take the pig. Do you think I'm stupid?"

Hargate spoke peremptorily.

"No Pulovski, no dropoff."

The line went dead.

Garcia reacted. "God damn it! This guy is serious!"

Hargate was not easily knocked down. "Listen to me," he said, "we've got no time, no money, and no leverage . . . don't you get it, Ray? Pulovski is already dead . . . he just doesn't know it."

The phone rang again and Garcia snatched it before Hargate could.

It was Strom. His voice was soft, suffused with menace.

"One more chance," he said, "you do as I say or the pig dies."

"Okay!" Garcia said. "Okay! we'll do it. But I want to hear Pulovski's voice . . . and I mean now."

The men in the room faintly heard Strom say: "Be smart."

"Nick," Garcia said, "Nick, are you there?"

"Yessir, Lieutenant, just sittin' tight."

"You goddamn fool. I told you to get off the case . . . but no, you had to be your stupid, stubborn, son-of-a-bitch self, and look where it got you!"

"I'm exactly where I want to be. Now you boys just stay home and save your money, and I'll take care of this myself."

There was a commotion, and Strom came on the line.

"You seem like an intelligent man . . . I hope you respect my capabilities more than your unreasonable friend here does."

The line went dead. Garcia held the phone in his hand, then turned to Hargate. Garcia shook his head, almost smiled.

"Sounds like Nick's got 'em outnumbered," he said lamely.

CHAPTER
25

—

AT around 8:30 the same morning Strom called, David Ackerman, astride the Harley, tooled down a hill in East Los Angeles.

Hopefully, he would get to Little Felix, and through him to Loco . . . and through Loco . . . Nick.

He knew that if he didn't reach Loco through Little Felix the game was likely over. What else could he do? Cops and FBI agents were combing the city for him. If they couldn't succeed, how could he?

But he did have one edge—and Pulovski would have approved. He didn't let the law get in his way. He remembered what Pulovski said of how real cops worked, and how they achieved what they had to any way they had to.

He almost smiled. He had once met an old ace homicide cop who had appalled him once when he said, half drunk, "I have committed many felonies in the pursuit of justice."

He was appalled then, but not now. It had been such a short time since he had been on auto theft, a raw rookie. He didn't feel like a rookie now. He was a son of a bitch, and he wondered who he reminded himself of.

Yes, he was Pulovski's best shot, just because he could do things other cops wouldn't do.

Welcome to the club, asshole.

The night before, he had run by the cleaners operated by Little Felix, "Limpio Vargas—Cleaners," and had learned that they opened at 8:30. He had debated whether or not to hit Little Felix before he got in the store, or after, and decided on after.

Ackerman was running a few minutes late—it was almost 8:35 when he arrived.

He pulled up and parked slightly down the block and approached the store on foot.

There was a sign on the door.

Shit.

It said CLOSED.

Maybe, Ackerman thought, someone had gotten to Little Felix. Warned him that a psycho cop was on the prowl for his ass. He might be long gone.

In frustration, Ackerman grabbed the door handle and shook it. He was surprised; the door opened.

He stepped inside.

The lights were off, but the light streaming in through the plate-glass windows in front afforded ample light.

It looked like any cleaning establishment. Counter, cash register, and, behind it, clothing on a couple of those carousel racks so popular today.

"Hello?" Ackerman called out.

No answer.

He decided to explore a little, but he also sensed danger. Maybe Little Felix was waiting for him, waiting to ambush him.

He unbuttoned his jacket and snapped the safety clip off the holster.

He scanned the area, then started walking to the left down a sort of pathway that led to the back.

He could not see or hear anything dangerous.

In the back was nothing much: a presser, a couple of machines for dry cleaning. The most prominent thing was the smell of the cleaning chemicals.

Then a sound, behind him.

He turned. The carousel was activated. Somebody had to be in the shop. He pulled his Beretta and started walking toward the front of the store.

The carousel kept moving as he did toward the front. He sensed great danger, but could not see it.

Then, out of the side of his eye he saw something that chilled him: Little Felix, in a clear plastic bag, hanging from one of the rack hooks. His tongue was out and bloated, his eyes fixed and dilated, and he was cyanotic and had lost control of his bowels and was very dead.

Ackerman tensed. The danger was palpable—and he sensed it just in time.

He put his hand up toward his face and for the moment that saved his life.

Loco had looped a wire garrote over his head but Ackerman's arm blocked it from going around his neck, which it would have cut through with relative ease.

It sliced into the hard muscle on Ackerman's forearm, Loco growling with the effort and Ackerman screaming with pain.

The struggle carried them to the front of the store near the counter so that they faced the back of the store.

Ackerman grabbed hold of the garrote, trying to relieve the pressure.

Through the intense pain, the huge strength of the man with the garrote, Ackerman knew that he would probably only get one shot at getting loose. He was still strong, but this kind of effort would soon leave him like a rag doll.

He lowered his head as far as he could, then brought it

back in a savage arc, smashing into Loco's face, then reached back and grabbed him by the hair and lifted his feet up, bracing them against the counter, and then pushed with all the fury and fear born of the instinct to survive.

They hurtled backward—and through the plate-glass window with a shattering crash and flopped onto the street, Loco losing his grip in the process.

Some Mexicans who lived on the street came running up.

Loco had pocketed the garrote and pointed to Ackerman. He spoke in Spanish.

"El mato Poquito Felix. El gringo maricón mato a el." Which meant: "He killed Little Felix and tried to kill me."

The small crowd looked in the store, and a few seconds later the carousel, still turning, came by showing Little Felix.

The crowd, furious, turned on Ackerman . . . and Loco slipped away.

Ackerman started to follow but was wrestled to the ground by the crowd, some of them yelling, *"Policia!* Somebody call the cops! *Policia."*

Ackerman, totally frustrated, screamed: "Let me go! I'm a fucking police officer! Get the hell off!"

The crowd, confused, relented—and Ackerman looked in the direction Loco had run. There was no sign of him.

God. All he could think about was Nick. What could he do now?

CHAPTER
26

HARGATE, Garcia, and a number of other cops spent the day after Strom's calls getting teams ready for the drop-off.

Of course they didn't have the money, but Hargate was sure of one thing. They were going to collar the dude who came to pick it up.

As the day wore on teams in the field searching for Pulovski came in with negative reports, and the FBI was having no luck. In Hargate's mind the game was over, but they would play it out until the end, if nothing else to forestall any criticism that they didn't do their best.

Garcia, meanwhile, had additional problems.

Now he was in his office and on the phone with a look of consternation on his face. He hung up and looked at Hargate.

"That's great. This is all I fuckin' need now."

Hargate, who had just come in after going home to freshen up, looked at him.

"Police brutality complaints have been coming from patrons of a bar in East LA all morning. Seems some cop assaulted a lot of people in it—and burned it to the ground. And the make on it makes it sound like Nick's partner, Ackerman.''

Hargate was surprised. He had Ackerman in his mind in one way: a yellow-bellied skunk.

''Acker . . . that goddamn rookie?''

Garcia nodded.

''I tried him at home. His girlfriend answered and she was worried as hell. Said he ran off last night . . . Hasn't heard from him since . . .''

Garcia thought a moment, then picked up the desk phone and punched out a number.

''Hey, Janovic,'' he said to Jerry Janovic, his assistant, ''round up a couple of people who know Ackerman's mug . . .''

''The rookie?''

''Yeah,'' Garcia affirmed, ''the new kid. Get 'em in unmarked cars and send 'em out looking for him. I want that fresh-faced punk picked up on sight.''

''Wang and Lance?''

''Yeah,'' Garcia said, ''Wang and Lance will do fine for starters.''

Garcia hung up. ''It's not just a job,'' he said to Hargate, ''it's a fuckin' adventure.''

CHAPTER
27

IF anything was needed to indicate the power of Eugene Ackerman, Sr., one could do worse than to just look at the Intertech Building headquarters in downtown Los Angeles.

It was a block of glass that stretched to the heavens and it was filled with people who, ultimately, had one main goal: make more money for Eugene Ackerman. And make it they did, a kind of private U.S. Mint that daily turned out an endless stream of greenbacks.

Eugene Ackerman had succeeded so phenomenally in business, he felt, in part, because of the image he projected. It was always positive, upbeat, professional. "Maybe you shouldn't judge a book by its cover," he was fond of saying, "but people do it all the time."

The building was part of that image, and so were the people who worked for him. He paid and treated his people well: he expected them to dress and act accordingly.

Furniture and furnishings had all been selected for their tasteful good looks and their power to impress.

But image for Ackerman went deeper. It was also intended to subtly intimidate, in the same essential way that movie producer Harry Cohn was said to intimidate by having his office chair and desk perched on a platform; unless you were Kareem Abdul Jabbar he would be looking down at you.

That's what Ackerman tried to accomplish too. Subtly, ever so subtly, he wanted people feeling a little cowed when they came into the offices of Intertech.

On the same morning that his son was engaged in a life or death struggle with Loco Martinez, Ackerman was in the boardroom sitting at the head of an oblong table.

The room itself was super impressive, flooring of wood blends that cost $70 a square foot, the rosewood paneling $150 each, the table, of book-matched veneers, $20,000 . . . and much more.

Arrayed around it were a dozen of his high-ranking executives. Each, in turn, was giving a weekly report on a particular phase of the operation of the company that others, then, would comment on and discuss—and sometimes argue about. Ackerman believed in a free flow of ideas and encouraged people to attack anyone—including himself.

Then from outside the massive doors that led to the room everyone in the conference room heard a commotion—someone talking loudly—and a moment later the doors burst open.

Eugene Ackerman's personal secretary was standing in the doorway. Standing in front of her was David Ackerman.

He was a mess.

There was the gash from the broken mirror, and the bruises and lacerations that had occurred from his two fights in La Casa Blanca. His shirt was torn and his arm covered with a makeshift bandage where Loco's garrote had cut into the flesh.

Most of all, though, he looked like a man possessed—and acted the part.

He walked into the room.

"Party's over. Everyone out of here."

The executives looked at one another, and wondered aloud just what in the hell was going on.

"What do you need," Ackerman said, "interoffice memos? *Shut up and get the hell out of here!*"

A glance from Eugene Ackerman told the executives what they wanted to know. Some grumbling, they filed out of the room.

When they were all out, David Ackerman closed the door behind them.

Eugene Ackerman stood up. "David . . . it's been all over the news . . . where the hell have you . . ."

His son cut in with a flat statement.

"I need two million dollars—in cash . . ."

His father looked at him, seemingly frozen . . .

". . . in four and a half hours," he concluded.

His father said nothing for a moment, then he did, his eyes troubled and sad.

"That's it, then. You keep making mistakes, and I go on paying for them."

David Ackerman felt a surge, a rage to say fuck you. But instead he headed for the door and opened it. Then he stopped, frozen, closed it and turned and went back into the room. He spoke, his voice low, thick with emotion.

"My partner is out there all alone. He is going to fucking die if I don't help. I'm the ballgame. I'm not coming to you because you're my father. I'm coming because you're the richest person I know."

Eugene Ackerman looked as if he had been physically cut. He went over to a massive liquor cabinet, extracted a Scotch bottle, and poured himself a drink.

"Who do you think," he said to his son, "you're punishing? Putting yourself out on the street, where you could be maimed or killed . . . I already lost one son, you can't know what that feels like."

"He was my brother," David said. "I know about that. I know. I know that a day has not gone by in my life when I don't mourn for him."

"You're my only son, goddammit . . . it's your responsibility to be there for us."

"*My responsibility? What about yours?* Where the hell were you when I was in pain . . . when I hurt?"

His father looked puzzled. "I always made sure you had everything you wanted."

David Ackerman's eyes filled with tears.

"Don't you know," he said softly but with paralyzing power, "that what I wanted most of all was you? You and Mom? But that you were never there to give me that. Were you angry with me? Did you blame me for Gene and didn't want to see me? I don't really know, Dad, and I don't fucking care anymore. I'm through making mistakes."

He paused, wiped his eyes. He said in an even, flat voice, "You couldn't buy me, Dad . . . but you can buy me time."

Eugene Ackerman had tears streaming down his face. He turned and went over to a window and looked out, then looked back.

"I'll do it with a condition. You forgive yourself. You do what you have to do, but when this is over you quit . . . give yourself a chance at a decent life. Is it a deal?"

David Ackerman shook his head. "No. This is my life. This is my job. This is my partner."

He paused. His voice was soft.

"Help me," he said, "please."

CHAPTER
28

I N the warehouse, Max and Cruz were downstairs, Max wielding a torch, working on the blue van, putting the finishing touches on a six-inch skirting. Upstairs on the third floor, standing near Pulovski, who was still tied to the chair, Liesl was about to work on her brain. She used a single-edge razor blade to separate a small pile of cocaine on a glass table into single lines, then used a golden straw to suck a line up through her nose.

Pulovski watched her with disapproval.

"Hey," he said, "I'm thirsty. Let me get a drink before you start in with that shit again."

Liesl eyed Pulovski. Her eyes were glazed. She glanced down at a pitcher of water on the table, then poured a glassful. Pulovski eyed the water being poured. He sensed something else was going on.

She walked over and stood opposite him. He got the idea. He opened his mouth and she put the glass to it and started to pour it in.

All the time, as he drank, they were looking at each other. Things were happening.

Pulovski finished all but the last swallowful. This he retained—and spit it in Liesl's face.

"Thanks," he said, smiling.

For a moment she was suffused with rage. Then her tongue snaked out and she licked some of the water that had dribbled down over her upper lip.

That sent a message to Pulovski.

She turned and went back to the table and picked up the razor blade. Pulovski couldn't help but notice how her ass and legs filled out her leather skirt.

She approached Pulovski, and smiled. He was smiling too.

"You're scared of me, aren't you?" he said. "You're scared of everyone when your charming boyfriend isn't around to watch your little ass, aren't you?"

Liesl grabbed Pulovski by the hair and pulled his head back, pulling his neck taut and exposed, the veins and arteries pulsating, prominent.

"You think you're a real man, don't you? A real American tough guy."

Keeping his head back, she brought the razor up to a point just below his eye. Pulovski was a statue. His eyelid twitched involuntarily.

"Pigs are all alike," Liesl said, "without their badges they're only half men, without their guns they're nothing at all . . . are you any different?"

Pulovski felt the strain of keeping his body tense, and he was aware that sweat was starting to form on his face, his heartrate increased.

"You'd better be," she continued, her voice low and suggestive, "because I hate anything useless. If something is no good to me I just cut it off and throw it away."

The sweat trickled down Pulovski's face.

Liesl leaned close, nose to nose, and slowly licked sweat from his face.

"You taste like fear, pig."

Pulovski was afraid, but he felt something else that warred with the fear. Lust. She was a beautiful woman, but perverse, animalistic, primitive. He hated her and she disgusted him. And he wanted to fuck her.

She moved her hand down to his groin and lay the razor on his knee.

She slid her hand on his penis, which was half erect. He moaned a little.

She continued to work on him, sliding her hand up and down his rapidly enlarging penis. His eyes closed momentarily, sweat pouring. He hated this but he couldn't help it. Lust had a mind of its own.

Then she stood up and walked to a VCR on the floor beside one of the monitors. A tape was sticking out of the VCR slot. She pushed it in and pressed RECORD.

Just like that, the image of Pulovski bound to the chair was shown on multiple screens, like lenses of a fly's eye.

She snaked her hand down inside her skirt toward her vagina and moved her hips sensually. Pulovski tried not to look at her. It was impossible.

"Now I'll have something to remember you by when you're dead," she said.

Her panties slid down her legs and pooled around her ankles. Grinding, eyeing Pulovski all the way, she stepped out of them. Now there was nothing beneath the skirt.

She approached Pulovski and straddled him, then lowered herself carefully onto his fully erect member.

Pulovski, ever the wiseguy, couldn't help but say, "So this is what is meant by going out with a bang."

Liesl, sweating, ground herself on Pulovski. Then she reached under her blouse and displayed a silver bullet on a chain around her neck.

"Our silver bullet. Erich wears an identical one. When one of us dies the other takes his own life with it. Romantic, no?"

Yeah, Pulovski thought, right out of Shakespeare.

She put the bullet against Pulovski's lips.

"Bite it."

Pulovski's mouth stayed closed.

Liesl picked the razor off his knee and raised it to his cheek. Pulovski got the message. He opened his mouth and bit the bullet.

Liesl, lust surging inside, then brought the razor down toward his penis and growled . . .

"Don't lose it, pig . . . don't lose it . . ."

Fear and lust warred in Pulovski.

Then Liesl was lost to lust, bucking and grinding furiously on Pulovski, and so was he. For just these moments he was just a man and she just a woman and moments later their muscles contracted and they emptied themselves into each other.

CHAPTER
29

AFTER meeting with his father, Ackerman called Sarah from the Intertech reception area. She was at his house and picked up the phone in the kitchen.

"Sarah?"

"David! My God . . . where are you?"

"It doesn't matter," he said. "Are you okay?"

"Am I okay . . . ? David, your parents have been calling all day . . . everyone's worried sick. Lieutenant Garcia is here . . . he says half the force is out looking for you."

"Everything's all right. I saw my father. Just stay with the lieutenant. Tell him I'll be there soon and explain everything."

"I'll tell him. I love you, David."

Ackerman nodded softly—he had such trouble telling people he loved them—then hung up the phone—and pulled out a small bottle of cheap Scotch. He poured a little on the bandage on his arm to provide just a little medication, then medicated himself with a quick swig.

Then he got an unpleasant surprise. Standing there were Lance and Wang, Cheech and Chong, both sporting shit-eating grins.

"Little early in the day for partying, ain't it, rookie?" Wang said.

Ackerman nodded.

"Let's take a hike," Lance said, "you're on our ten most wanted list."

Christ, Ackerman thought, they were nasty shits. But he left with them.

At the house, after she hung up, Sarah went into the living room where the lieutenant was watching television. He was sitting on the couch, his back turned to her, smoking.

"Lieutenant," Sarah said, "that was David. He said he'll be here shortly."

Loco Martinez turned and smiled at Sarah.

"That's great. Thank you, Sarah."

CHAPTER
30

LOCO Martinez, despite his savage appearance, was not just muscle. He was devious, a street-smart killer who used whatever he could to gain an edge on an opponent.

Information was part of what he tried to gather. Snippets of information that might pay off one day in unexpected ways.

Which was exactly why he was at David Ackerman's house now. During the fight with the cop at the bar, he had taken his wallet, and knew where Ackerman lived. And he knew how to use that information . . .

Loco had iced Little Felix based on a tip from one of the bikers at La Casa Blanca, who had overheard Ackerman trying to get Loco's name, and then getting Little Felix's.

Little Felix knew too much about Loco—and Strom—to be allowed to live.

But then the cop had spotted him at the scene and therefore, in Loco's mind, became dead meat. He didn't want people running around who could put him at a murder scene, particularly a cop. Ackerman had to go.

He had arrived at the house barely twenty minutes earlier. He was going to break in but Ackerman's gash was there.

He could have clipped her outright, but he enjoyed the game. He had seen Garcia on TV, knew Ackerman was being sought. It was easy to make believe he was Garcia. If she had known he wasn't Garcia, he would have killed her on the spot, maybe fucked her too.

This way, though, she would live a little longer. And it was always a good idea to think things through as much as you could before acting.

Now, Sarah called to him from the kitchen. "Is decaf okay, Lieutenant? David hates caffeine."

"Decaf is fine. But don't worry, a couple more years and David'll be a speed freak like us old-timers. Hey, do you mind if I look around?"

"Be my guest, Lieutenant."

"Just call me Ray."

Then Loco went to the wall and yanked the phone connection out of the jack and started to explore. He wanted to make sure there was nothing here that could hurt him. He was going to be the one doing the hurting.

CHAPTER
31

OUTSIDE Intertech, Lance and Wang, flanking David Ackerman, walked him across the street toward the unmarked car they had parked there.

"Christ . . ." Lance said, "I don't know what you've been up to, Ackerman, but Garcia is pissing fire . . . wants you downtown like last Thursday."

These guys, Ackerman thought, were not only nasty but misinformed.

"Garcia isn't at headquarters," Ackerman said.

Lance opened the back of the car. "Sure as shit is. We just spoke to him before we came to pick you up. He called from headquarters."

The realization dawned quickly, and he suddenly felt breathless, very afraid. His wallet. He had never gotten it back. They knew where he lived.

"Oh, my God . . . *Oh, my God . . . I've got to get home!*"

"No way, kiddo. You're coming downtown right now," Wang said.

Lance continued to guide him through the door to the back seat. Ackerman seemed relaxed, but inside he was a ball of intensity. He had to make a move before it was too late.

He moved.

He slipped the handcuffs off Lance's belt . . .

"What the hell," Lance said.

. . . and just that quick Ackerman, fast and strong, had one of the cuffs locked on Lance's wrist and punched him hard in the stomach, immobilizing him.

Then Wang moved toward him and Ackerman brought his elbow against his face with punishing force. Wang went down, dazed, and in that moment Ackerman slid the cuff through the doorhandle and then snapped it on Wang's wrist.

Lance was starting to recover. Ackerman pushed him back, then went through their pockets, found the keys and tossed them down a nearby sewer.

The whole operation had taken thirty seconds, though it seemed like forever.

Sarah's life was on the line. Somebody wanted him out of the way—and Sarah was expendable.

Ten seconds later Ackerman was roaring down the block on the Harley, acting as if there were no other traffic, no lights, no pedestrians . . . nothing.

To him, now, there wasn't. There was just Sarah.

Then, almost predictably, there was a traffic jam, which he got around by powering down the yellow line between the lines of traffic at sixty miles an hour.

He knew that he was taking his life in his hands. But that was a risk. He knew that if he didn't arrive on time Sarah had no chance at all.

CHAPTER
32

IN the bedroom, as he "looked around," Loco made another important discovery. Another phone. He disabled it.

"Nice place you got here," he called to Sarah in the kitchen.

And then, as quietly as he could, he closed one window, then another, and locked both.

Out of the bedroom, he discovered a back door and locked it. There were some appliances near the back door.

"Dryer and everything," he said toward the kitchen where Sarah was still busy. "Me, I got to go to the cleaners. I was just there, as a matter of fact."

And he smiled, relishing the irony.

In the kitchen Sarah spooned out the instant coffee into a cup, then poured boiling water in it. She placed the cup on a saucer, then gathered cream and sugar on a small tray and exited the kitchen and went into the living room.

The room was empty, the only sign of life the television

where, she half realized, they were talking about the Pulovski kidnaping again.

Lieutenant Garcia was nowhere in sight. Where was he? Probably still in the bathroom or bedroom.

Come to think of it, she thought, why would he want to look around? What did that have to do with anything?

Then she was distracted by something on the television, something that for a moment her mind was unable to put together.

The announcer had introduced someone . . . someone named Lieutenant Ray Garcia.

". . . We were on the scene right after the shocking events, and managed to talk to the lieutenant in charge of the kidnaped officer's division, Raymond Garcia. His comments were quite unorthodox . . . ."

The real Garcia appeared, and Sarah was confused.

But, Sarah thought, that was impossible: Lieutenant Garcia was here.

And then she put it together and gooseflesh bloomed and she sensed rather than saw someone behind her and as she turned Loco Martinez, malevolent and smiling, looked down on her, garrote in his hands . . .

She threw the hot coffee in his face and he screamed in agony and threw his hands up to his face and Sarah ran to the front door . . . and it was locked.

It only took Loco a moment to recover and he was after her again.

He grabbed her and tossed her away from the door and back into the living room. Sarah, terrified, grabbed the phone off the table and brought it into Loco's face with all the force she could muster, but it had little effect and he punched her in the chest. The phone fell to the floor, and then he had her. He got her by the hair and pulled her back savagely, exposing her slim neck, holding her tight. She was helpless.

"For this, *puta*," he said, "I'm going to make it hurt."

He started to loop the garrote around her neck when David Ackerman came through the front door without opening it on the Harley at thirty miles an hour, shredding it like balsa wood, the bike crashing to a stop at the living-room wall, Ackerman diving free just before it did.

A moment later he had the stunned Loco by the legs and he went down. They thrashed, punched, kicked, rolled along the floor.

Sarah shrieked, terrified, but through the fear she remembered that David had another gun . . . an automatic . . .

She raced to the bedroom, ripped open dresser doors, searched frantically for the gun.

The fight, meanwhile, had spilled into the kitchen.

Loco slammed Ackerman against the refrigerator and in turn Ackerman kicked him, like a jackhammer, in the chest, sending him sprawling backward, and he reached into the sink and brought up a big knife.

Ackerman knew that with a streetfighter like Loco handling a knife he was in deep trouble. For a moment they stood frozen, looking at each other, and then Loco lunged . . .

The first shot hammered into his stomach but hardly slowed him down. The second shot went through his heart.

Sarah stood in the doorway, watching him fall, her arms extended, the .25 automatic held with both hands.

For a moment they were absolutely still, ears ringing, a trace of cordite smoke trailing across the kitchen . . .

Then Sarah lowered the gun.

Ackerman went over and checked Loco, then looked at Sarah. Then it dawned on him what Loco's death meant.

"I needed him alive, damn it!"

Sarah had started to seriously shake—and anger surged.

"Then I should have let him kill you," she said.

"If I had wanted him dead I would have shot him myself."

Tears formed in Sarah's eyes.

Ackerman went back to Loco's body. He frisked him—
and came out with his wallet and shield. He sighed.

He went close to Sarah.

"Maybe next time aim for his kneecaps," he said.

"I was," Sarah said.

Ackerman took her in his arms and embraced her. Her head
rested against his chest and he comforted her—but part of
him still wanted Loco alive . . .

And then his pulse spurted. As he looked out the doorway
he noticed something that had been hidden behind another
parked car when he came blasting through. It was the nose
of a car and it had thunderous, wonderful significance.

The nose belonged to the gruesome green Lotus that Loco
drove, which Ackerman had first spotted in the warehouse
the day he and Pulovski went to visit Max . . .

He went up to the doorway. Sarah followed. He said something that indicated he was very happy but that totally puzzled
her.

"Anyone who could deface a work of art like that . . .
oughta be shot."

CHAPTER
33

STROM, dressed in a gray worker's jumpsuit, stood in the repair shop area of the warehouse and looked at the two vans. The work was complete and they looked good.

Max had put a seamless skirting on the blue van, and AVCO AIR COURIER had been carefully painted on both sides of the white one.

It was all part of a plan that he had worked out quickly but he thought should beat the pigs if they tried to double-cross him. And he thought they might. That was okay. If Cruz could pick up the money, Strom would win—the plan was that good. If they simply arrested him and didn't fork over the money, that would be bad, but he and Liesl could start over. He was too good at what he did not to succeed.

Either way, of course, the cop was dead.

His plan, then, was not one hundred percent airtight, though this didn't bother him. In fact, he sort of liked it. It put an edge on the whole thing. It was why he was at the pickup spot when the cop showed up. If he hadn't been, they wouldn't have had as much trouble with the cop. But some part of him did not regret it, and he liked the idea of killing the *shvartze*.

Liesl was the same way. She liked risk, got off on it. He had seen that on a number of occasions. When it was risky, and they had killed, it would turn them into sexual beasts. They could fuck and suck all night, both tapping pools of sexual potency in each other that it was sometimes hard to believe existed.

He knew she had fucked the cop, but that didn't bother him. That was perverse, bizarre, something else that turned her on.

It was the same with him. If it had been a female cop, he would have fucked her until she came. Then he would have killed her, and he and Liesl would have fucked to the memory of the cop dying.

He would get some residual enjoyment out of Liesl having fucked Pulovski. Later, he would fuck her, his cock driving into the same place as the dead cop, partly lubricated by the dead man's juices.

Strom smiled slightly, his large liquid eyes glittering, and he felt a little aroused. Ain't life grand, he thought.

His thoughts were interrupted by Max walking into the shop. He had been on a little errand. He took his sunglasses off as he came closer.

"The van's in place, Mr. Strom."

Strom checked his Rolex: 6:45. On schedule, so far.

"Good," Strom said. "Max, get up there, get your car, help Liesl with the pig, and then you're out of here."

Max nodded and immediately turned and headed for the stairwell.

Strom turned toward the stiletto man, Cruz, who had been standing by smoking.

Like Strom, he was dressed in a gray jumpsuit. Ever the fashion plate, he wore a Dodger baseball cap.

"All right," Strom said to him, "get ready."

Cruz was a little confused. Loco hadn't arrived.

"What about Loco?"

"Loco hasn't called in. You handle it yourself and I save fifty grand. *Move*."

Cruz thought that it was okay. Maybe Strom would give him a bonus, part of the money he would have paid Loco.

He got in the blue van and started the engine. It purred.

Strom, meanwhile, adjusted an H & K automatic he had shoved down in his belt and picked up two Uzis from the table as well as boxes of extra shells. He placed the guns and ammunition in the passenger seat of the white van.

Yes, he thought, this was going to be exciting.

CHAPTER
34

LIESL, also dressed in a gray jumpsuit, a .357 Magnum jammed down in the belt around her slim waist, was just finishing pushing her hair up under a small cap when Max emerged from the stairwell.

"We're movin', babe."

Liesl smiled. Good.

"Which one do you want?" Liesl said, referring to the black or white Mercedes, the only vehicles on the floor that had not been completely or partially chopped.

Max grinned, his eyes got wide. He loved cars as much as he loved women—and talked about them the same way.

"This beauty here," he said, pointing to the white one, "oughta do me just fine."

Liesl picked up some bags from one of the glass tables and carried them over and handed them to Max. He got into the car and a moment later the engine was idling.

Liesl walked back to where Pulovski was.

She looked at his battered face, which was covered with a heavy growth of beard. He looked totally out of it.

But his swollen eyes opened slightly and he brightened when he saw it was Liesl.

"Going on a little trip, are we?"

Liesl looked at him. She felt power surge. He was so helpless.

"Pity you won't see the sights," she said as she pulled the .357 from her belt and casually but effectively slammed it across Pulovski's temple. His head dropped to his chest like a rag doll's, as if all his neck muscles had suddenly been severed.

She eyed him for a millisecond, then bent down and untied his feet from the chair. His hands were bound but not attached.

"Come on, Max," she called. Pulovski was way too big for her to handle alone, particularly dead weight.

She leaned down and grabbed him under his arm and then his head suddenly snapped up furiously, caught her on the chin, and she fell over backward, the gun falling out of her hand and skittering along the floor . . . and she collided with the VCR, activating it, and all the screens jumped to life, showing Liesl lifting her leather skirt, about to slide down onto Pulovski . . . complete with the sound . . .

" . . . Now I'll have something to remember you by when you're dead."

Pulovski was not, at that moment, interested in reviewing the tape.

In a millisecond he was on his back and with effort born of savage desperation was able to hunch himself up and pass his bound hands over his feet, putting them in front of him.

In a few seconds Liesl was on her feet and on him. She delivered a stinging punch to Pulovski's face, then swung at him with a vicious, 360-degree karate kick that connected— snagged by the rope that bound his hands.

Pulovski gave her a vicious twist and her head landed on the concrete with a satisfying and sickening thump, knocking her unconscious. Pulovski smiled as he disentangled himself.

"Chill or die, motherfucker."

Pulovski glanced over sharply.

Max was out of the car and had Liesl's .357 leveled at him.

Pulovski knew Max, and he knew something else. He started walking toward him. He spoke through clenched teeth.

"I don't think so, boy—some very nasty person we know might not take it too kindly if you blew away his meal ticket . . ."

Max didn't know what to do. He backed away, trying to decide.

"You don't want to be putting two million dollars' worth of merchandise in the garbage, do you, boy?"

Max decided to pull the trigger but he was a hair too late. Pulovski knocked the gun from his hands, simultaneously kneeing him in the groin, and Max flopped facedown on the floor.

Pulovski jumped for the gun—but Max still had life . . . he squirmed to it and slapped it. It skittered along the floor and disappeared down the open elevator shaft a few yards away.

Pulovski expressed his appreciation by kicking Max in the mouth, knocking five teeth out in the process.

Pulovski thought the fight was over and headed for the stairwell, and then he was down again, Max having tackled him, and Max pummeled Pulovski and then Pulovski got the cord binding his hands looped over Max's head and onto his neck and choked him savagely.

Max, in turn, elbowed Pulovski in the stomach and he went down, on his back and then up and over, Max flying in the air, and when he hit the floor Pulovski heard the satisfying sound of his spine snapping.

And then he felt the less satisfying feeling of being pulled somewhere. He turned and realized that Max was falling in the open elevator shaft—and pulling him with him.

Pulovski fought it, knowing that if he went with Max it was bye-bye, but Max was dead weight hanging in the shaft and he struggled desperately, trying to use arm strength and his body weight as a counterweight to Max, but then felt himself being pulled closer and closer to the shaft and his last thought was "Shit" as Max went down the shaft, Pulovski in tow . . .

CHAPTER
35

DOWN in the auto repair shop, Cruz, sitting in the blue van, was revving the engine—and raring to go. He looked at Strom, who was sitting behind the wheel of the white van.

Strom nodded, and Cruz put the van in gear and was off.

Strom looked at his watch. Liesl and Max were late . . . and the elevator that would transport the car Max would use hadn't moved.

"Goddamn," he said out loud.

Then it occurred to him. Maybe Max had trouble with the car. But there were *two* cars there. He could take either one.

A few moments earlier he thought he had heard a thumping sound but couldn't be sure because Cruz was revving the engine.

Just as a precaution, because it was the way he was, he

picked one of the Uzis off the passenger seat and got out of
the van. He walked toward the elevator.

He got on the elevator, a large freight elevator some twenty
by twenty-five feet, closed the accordion-fold safety gate,
and pressed the start button on the control panel inside the
elevator.

The elevator clanked and groaned, and started moving upward with a grinding sound.

Directly above Strom, on the open grill paneling that
formed the ceiling of the elevator, were two other passengers.

Max, whose body had been battered and mashed in the
fall, was lying facedown.

Pulovski was directly on top of Max, as if cornholing him.
Pulovski was alive, thanks to Max's body serving as a human
buffer when they—or Max—slammed into the grillwork.

Pulovski was alive—and awake—well aware when Strom
got on the elevator . . . but there was simply nothing he could
do about it . . .

And then he spotted it, only two feet away, the .357 that
Max had knocked down the shaft. If he could get to that . . .

He was able to disentangle himself from Max's neck, then
started to crawl toward the gun . . .

Unknown to Pulovski, a drop of Max's blood had splattered
on the elevator floor, right next to Strom . . .

With great effort, any noise drowned out by the elevator
sounds, Nick crawled and crawled and . . . he gripped the
pleasant cold handle of the gun . . .

Everytime it rains, it rains gunfire from heaven, he hummed
to himself.

He looked down at Strom's loathsome black head and
shoulders and poked the barrel of the .357 through the grill
and was unaware that just at that moment another drop of
blood fell from Max but this time splattered on Strom's shoulder and he looked up just before Nick squeezed the trigger

and saw the barrel of the gun and dived out of the way just as the gun exploded.

The shot missed.

Pulovski shot again but the angle was difficult and he missed and he did not get a third shot—Strom had torn the safety door open and jumped out of the elevator as it passed the second-floor opening.

The elevator continued up while Strom ran to the stairwell and yelled as he went up, three steps at a time.

"Liesl! Liesl!"

She had regained consciousness and was well aware of what was happening and was way ahead of Strom. As Strom ran onto the warehouse floor Liesl was at the control panel there and Strom heard the elevator come to a grinding halt.

"It's the cop!" she said. "He's trapped."

Strom walked over to the elevator shaft, looked down. He caught a glimpse of Pulovski.

"Hey, cop."

Pulovski responded with a shot from the .357, just missing Strom. Strom shut the safety gate.

"Are you listening to me?" he said.

Pulovski was listening—and waiting.

He could see the short, nasty barrel of the Uzi poking through the gate.

"I really don't have time for this, cop. I wanted to keep you as insurance but at this hour it really doesn't matter. If you want to live for a few more hours, put down that gun."

Pulovski answered with silence. He knew that, essentially, he was a sitting duck. He knew also that he was at the end of the road with this asshole.

Strom started to squeeze the trigger to spray the grill when he was interrupted by a bullet that smashed into the wall two inches from his skull.

He whirled.

David Ackerman was standing by the stairwell, legs bent,

arms extended in combat firing position. He squeezed off another shot . . . But Strom brought up the Uzi and squeezed off a nasty burst, making Ackerman dive out of the way and behind a chopped car, and Strom jumped behind another cannibalized car.

Then someone screamed and Ackerman looked up and there on all the TV monitors was a high point of the Liesl-Pulovski film with Liesl riding Pulovski and screaming and then suddenly one of the monitors exploded as Strom fired again.

Ackerman returned fire as Strom yelled to Liesl . . . "Get out of here!"

She did. Strom covered her exit out the door with a stream of fire.

Then, intermittently firing, he raced the few short steps to the control panel, pressed UP, and as the elevator started toward the roof, Strom jumped back down behind the car and then deliberately blasted the control panel to pieces. Sweaty, as animated as he ever got, he experienced a deep sense of satisfaction of a single sound: The elevator had kept going up.

He reloaded, then covered himself with bursts as he ran for and made the stairwell.

On the elevator, Pulovski knew that it would stop—only after he and Max had been waffled by the grill. And he wasn't too clear how the fuck he was going to get out. I wait, he thought, for suggestions.

Ackerman understood Pulovski's predicament very clearly. When Strom left he raced to the control panel but there was nothing to press: it was a ganglion of shattered parts and wires.

Then the elevator moved up to the third-floor opening.

Pulovski was momentarily distracted from the prospect of dying when he saw Ackerman standing futilely at the control panel.

"What the hell are you doing here? *You're supposed to be dead!*"

Ackerman did not answer. Instead he raced over and tore open the safety gate—and Pulovski jumped off with little or no space to spare, flopping on the floor.

A few moments later a grinding sound was heard as the elevator contacted the cable reels, framework and assorted machinery at the top. Pulovski, still down, grimaced as Ackerman answered his question.

"I never do what I'm supposed to, remember?"

Eyeing the stairwell door, gun trained on it in case someone returned, Ackerman helped Pulovski to his feet.

Pulovski was suffused with gratefulness that Ackerman had saved his life. Sure.

"This is twice," Pulovski said, "you've let me down, kid, but I think I'll cut you some slack this time. Where's your backup?"

Ackerman didn't answer. Instead he raised Pulovski's wrists, placed the muzzle against the rope, and fired, severing it.

He looked at Pulovski, a twinkle in his eyes. "You're my backup."

Pulovski nodded. This kid, he thought as he checked the .357 for ammunition, was getting to be a real wise ass. But he had big balls.

"You know, kid, if you weren't such a smart-ass bastard I could almost get to like you."

Then Pulovski noticed the monitors and went over to them quickly and turned them off, the screens instantly showing the various areas within the warehouse again.

"Wait a minute, I was enjoying that," Ackerman said.

"Not as much as I was."

Then Pulovski noticed on one of the monitors the white van scooting across the ground floor and out of the monitor's field of vision.

Something clicked in his brain that made his stomach tighten.

Max. Max behind the monitors, the shit about redrawing the maps to the area . . . then the nightmare came home . . .

In the white van Strom was going to make the nightmare come true. He picked up the remote control device and started to tap in a numbered sequence. "All right, you troublesome bastards," he said.

Inside the warehouse Pulovski had run to the white Mercedes that Max was going to take. It was still idling. "We've got to get out of here . . ." Pulovski yelled.

"The stairs are . . ."

But Pulovski wasn't listening. He was in the car and slammed it into drive and put the accelerator to the floor, squealing across it and burning rubber as he stopped next to the totally confused Ackerman.

"*Get in, kid, now*," Pulovski barked.

Ackerman was barely in when Pulovski slammed the stick into reverse and backed up dementedly.

He stopped, looked at Ackerman. "Fasten your fucking seat belt." His eyes were shagging flies without a glove.

"Are you fucking crazy?"

Pulovski put the hammer to the floor, headed toward one of the glass walls of the warehouse, remembering that it overlooked the roof of a smaller warehouse and thinking, also, that if he wanted to live dangerously, it didn't get any better than this. He would be successful or he and the kid would bypass ICU and go direct to the fucking bone orchard.

Ackerman screamed as the car blasted through the wall, three heartbeats before Strom brought his thumb down on the remote's final number and said: "Have a blast."

The car was airborne, free of the building, when it went up. The shock wave buffeted the car that one and a half seconds later landed with an ass-jarring crunch on the adjacent warehouse roof and then Ackerman screamed again as the car, as if on ice, slid across the tar-paper roof and smashed into a big doghouse-style skylight and then dipped and did a submarine dive into *that* warehouse until it collided, twenty feet later, with a huge pile of old washing machines and driers and came to a stop, right side up.

Pulovski looked with chagrin at the kid.

"I told you to fasten that."

Ackerman did not answer for a moment. He did not know if he was alive. He would find out when he tried to speak.

"You all right, kid?"

"I don't know. Are we done yet?"

Pulovski opened the car door and started to climb down. Ackerman followed.

"We aren't done . . . but *you* are."

"What the hell is that supposed to mean?"

They had reached floor level.

"I mean you did a real good job back there and I'm grateful to ya, but I'm going after that son of a bitch and I don't need you watching my back."

"Oh, yeah. Well, while you were up there playing house with Ms. Hitler . . ."

"Don't knock it 'til you've tried it."

". . . I was out busting my ass and half of the goddamn city to save your stupid hide. I'm liable to get arrested by the first cop that lays eyes on me."

"You have the right to remain silent. You have the right to a . . ."

"*Fuck you, Nick.*"

Pulovski turned and started to walk out of the warehouse. Ackerman followed.

"Don't worry, I'm sure your old man'll have no problem bailing you out."

Ackerman grabbed Pulovski by the shoulder, whirled him around, and threw a right cross—which was caught by Pulovski's hand. They glared at each other, then Ackerman relaxed his arm.

"My old man was ready to bail you out . . . two million dollars . . . for your ass."

Pulovski let go of Ackerman's hand.

"You tell him I'm mighty obliged."

"He didn't do it for you . . . he did it for me. *I* did it for you."

Finally Pulovski understood, and even he had no wisecrack to make. And then he and Ackerman walked silently out of the warehouse—together.

CHAPTER
36

THE street where the pickup was to be made by a man in a blue van was barricaded at both ends and loaded for bear. There were SWAT sharpshooters on the rooftops, motorcycle cops and a bunch of black and whites at either end of the barricades, and, circling in the sky, two choppers equipped with powerful searchlights.

Hargate, who was the chief architect of the scene, was parked in an unmarked car at one end of the street. The futility of it all struck him, however, once he saw it all in place.

"This is ridiculous," he said to his driver. "We'll never see that cop alive again . . . we shouldn't even be here. Nobody's going to show."

Hargate was wrong.

Exactly two minutes later his driver spotted the blue van. It was at the far end of the block from where Hargate was. He spoke into the mike: "That's it. Let him in."

The barricades were pulled apart and the van moved slowly between them and stopped in the middle of the block.

Then Cruz, the driver, stepped out, his face flattened, distorted by a nylon stocking he had pulled over it.

Hargate barked into the mike: "Move in and grab the son of a . . . wait . . ."

Hargate stopped speaking. A white Lincoln limo had pulled into the street, then had stopped at the barricades. Someone in the limo spoke to the people manning the barricades—and was let through.

The rear door opened and out stepped Ray Garcia, followed by Eugene Ackerman, who carried a black suitcase.

Hargate couldn't believe it.

"What the . . . Ray?"

Cruz stepped back as Garcia handed him the suitcase.

Cruz glanced suspiciously at Garcia and Ackerman, then placed the case on the street and opened it. It was filled with money.

Satisfied, he snapped the case shut and stood up. He stepped back into the van. A helicopter hovering above shone the searchlight on the car with a light as bright as daylight.

Inside his unmarked car, Hargate debated what to do. They had obviously given him the money.

He decided to play it out the way Strom had instructed them. But they would have to be very, very careful. They couldn't lose that van.

Inside the van, the tinted windows giving him privacy, Cruz opened an attaché case and pulled out a portable phone. He dialed the number.

It rang inside the white van that was moving toward the freight end of LA International Airport. Strom was driving, Liesl in the passenger seat.

She picked up. "Well?" she said.

"It's all here. I'm on my way."

Meanwhile Garcia had gotten into Hargate's car.

"We just bought two million dollars' worth of time," he said. And thought: I hope.

Hargate was focused on the blue van.

"He's moving! Let's get this goddamn show rolling!"

The van moved slowly along the street, making no attempt to evade the road show that was monitoring his progress—black and whites, motorcycles and the chopper overhead that kept him fixed in the light.

Cruz knew that he didn't have to. He smiled. Were they going to get an unpleasant surprise.

Two blocks beyond the barricade, he got one himself.

Screeching out of the darkness of a side street was Loco's green Lotus—which smacked into the driver's side of the van.

Ackerman and Pulovski burst out, blood in their eyes.

Pulovski ripped open the door and Ackerman jumped in, saying hello by smashing Cruz in the face. They pushed Cruz out of the way, Pulovski got in the driver's seat and got the van rolling.

"I knew," Pulovski said, "that green mutation was good for something."

Cruz blinked. "You . . ." he said to Ackerman. "You . . . I saw you die."

"Welcome to hell, asshole," Pulovski said.

Garcia and Hargate had been observing the little drama from Hargate's car. Garcia was jubilant.

"Nick! That was Nick!"

"What the hell was he doing?"

"I don't know, but we're sure as shit going to back him up on it."

CHAPTER
37

O UTSIDE the blue van, the phalanx of cops followed. Inside the blue van, it wasn't Cruz's day.

Ackerman rifled his pockets, emerged with his stiletto, and used it to slice off the nylon mask, revealing a wide-eyed heavily sweating Cruz made more sweaty when he became aware that Ackerman had placed the point of the blade under his chin, perhaps to drive it northward.

"There's a turn coming up," Ackerman said to Cruz. "You say left or right. One mistake and you get a smile you'll keep for the rest of your short life."

Cruz felt like farting when Ackerman pressed the point a little farther into his chin—it was close to breaking the skin.

"Right . . . right, man, right . . ."

Pulovski made the turn and looked at Ackerman.

"What've you been, rehearsing that shit?"

"I'm done rehearsing."

He grinned into Cruz's face.

"Good boy," Ackerman said. "Now I know Strom would

never send you out without an escape route planned. We're gonna lose the cops, understand?"

Cruz said nothing. He hated this gringo puta motherfucker, but he was very afraid of him too. But they had pushed him too motherfucking far. He had decided not to cooperate. He looked fierce, and fiercely determined.

Inside, Pulovski had started to glow. The kid was picking up real fast. Perhaps he was ready for graduate school.

"You're sounding pretty good there, kid, but are you ready to take the next step?"

"I don't know, what is it?"

Pulovski looked at Cruz like he was used toilet tissue.

"Killing an uncooperative asshole in cold blood."

Cruz had to exercise all his willpower to keep from doing a double in his underwear.

"I'd say," Pulovski said, "this is as good a time as any."

Ackerman nodded and pressed the knife even harder into Cruz's chin.

"Stop!" Cruz cried. "I'll do it . . . I'll fucking do it."

Ackerman pulled the knife back.

"Crazy motherfuckers, man, crazy mother . . ."

Pulovski's elbow interfaced with Cruz's jaw at high speed.

"Watch your language, you sack of shit," Pulovski cautioned.

The caravan of cops continued to follow, and at one point the van, after making a right turn, slowed and stopped at a red light. The searchlight was still on it.

Hargate and Garcia watched it carefully. Neither man had said a word in the last three minutes because of the danger of it distracting their attention.

The light turned green, then red again . . .

Something was wrong.

"They're not moving," Hargate said, "what's going on?"

"Who the hell knows," Garcia said.

They waited one more light change and then Hargate gave the order to move in.

Cops engulfed the van and pried the rear door open. Hargate and Garcia looked in. It was dimly lit.

And empty. There were some cardboard boxes in the back, but other than that—empty.

Garcia and Hargate thought the same thing: Where the fuck were they?

Hargate went into the van and booted aside the cardboard boxes. The answer was in the floor.

There was a bail handle attached to what might be a trapdoor. Garcia, who had joined Garcia inside the vehicle, pulled the trapdoor up.

"Oh, Christ," Hargate said.

Directly beneath the trapdoor was a manhole cover, partly off.

Garcia looked at the manhole.

Christ, he thought, never a dull moment with Nick Pulovski. He just hoped that whatever he was going to do he would return in one piece.

CHAPTER
38

A BOUT a minute after Garcia and Hargate learned how the occupants had gotten out of the van, a couple of rats in an alley not too far away were unceremoniously disturbed by the movement of another manhole cover. A moment later Cruz emerged, followed by Ackerman and Pulovski.

Cruz and Ackerman shoved the heavy metal circle back in place.

Stealthily they emerged at the head of the alley and peeked both ways. No one.

Across the street was their destination, yet a third van, this also white with AVCO AIR COURIER emblazoned on the side, parked at a curb, a mirror image of the one Strom and Liesl were using at the airport.

"Hey," Pulovski said as they trotted across the street, "this is a pretty good plan. Strom did himself proud."

Pulovski and Ackerman grinned. Cruz was in a less merry mood.

At the van Ackerman said to Cruz: "Give him the keys."

Cruz dutifully handed Pulovski the van's keys. Pulovski, using a sixteen-shot Beretta as a directional aid, motioned Cruz to get in on the passenger side. He did.

Ackerman got in on the other side of Cruz, making him the filling in a very uncomfortable sandwich, and a few seconds later Pulovski had the engine purring and the van moving down the block.

As they went, Ackerman picked up the case holding the portable telephone.

"This thing," he said to Cruz, "wasn't in the other van for decoration. You've been calling in. Call now. Let's see what they have to say."

"They been calling me."

"Bullshit," Pulovski snarled.

Then Cruz looked cross-eyed up at the stiletto, the point of which Ackerman had placed between his eyes. He winced, looked away—and then did a super wince as Ackerman brought the knife down and doodled it against his crotch. Cruz's expression indicated a sense of cooperation.

"If I even *think* you're pulling some fast shit on me, I'm gonna cut it off and let you live to remember how good it felt."

Pulovski solved the matter of Cruz dialing the phone. He picked it up and pressed redial. Who else, he had thought, could this hump be likely to call?

The phone rang and Liesl, still in the other AVCO van, picked up.

"Yeah?"

"Cruz."

"You're behind schedule. What's going on?"

"There was a delay, but I'm cool. I'll be there in fifteen."

"Ten," Liesl said, and hung up.

Pulovski glanced over and saw that Ackerman still had the knife by Cruz's privates. He grimaced.

"Kid," he said, "don't even joke about that."

CHAPTER
39

THE Falcon 20 jet was parked in the same place it had been the night before when the pilot, Blackwell, had called Strom, irked that he was not ready to go.

Though it was around ten P.M., the airport was still busy, the huge 747s and 767s and LT-10s coming in from literally all over the world. It was an airport that never closed.

It was also an airport that, particularly in the present climate, made security a priority. Security personnel, both uniformed and plainclothes, had been instructed to sin on the side of aggressiveness. They prowled the facility, their eyes constantly searching for trouble—or potential trouble.

Erich Strom knew this, and it was why he and Liesl were suitably outfitted in uniforms and the van they drove seemed to be legitimate.

Still, nothing is perfect, and when Erich Strom pulled the air courier van near the Falcon 20, he suddenly found himself, as he exited the vehicle, caught in the lights of a security vehicle. Two young uniformed guards, both wearing side arms, got out of the vehicle and approached him.

Strom knew he had trouble. He had no authorization to be on the field and he did not have phony ID.

He stopped and smiled in a friendly way.

"Can I help you?" he said.

The taller of the two guards smiled.

"We're going to run a routine check on your cargo, sir."

Strom nodded and stepped back, offering them free access to the back of the van.

One of the guards swung the doors open.

Liesl was crouched in the darkness. A smile played on her lips and then she squeezed the trigger of the Uzi she held and raked across the guards with a silenced burst of bullets. The bullets chewed up their bodies and they were virtually jetting blood before they hit the ground.

It was always a wonder how with such little noise so much mayhem could be done.

Liesl lay the Uzi down and then she and Strom picked up the bodies, and, in turn, loaded them into the van and then closed the doors. Then Strom drove the van seventy-five yards away and walked back to the Falcon.

He checked his watch as he went. Cruz should be here soon, he thought.

They went up the stairs into the Falcon.

Blackwell was in the pilot's seat. Strom entered and sat down next to him.

"Are we ready?" Strom asked.

"Two minutes," Blackwell said.

Two minutes later Blackwell started the plane. The jet's turbo engines started to whine, then coughed to life and the twin props revved.

Strom and Liesl looked across the field.

Now all they had to do was wait for the van—and two million dollars.

CHAPTER
40

THE noise, inside the Falcon 20, was literally deafening, hitting a decibel level that was about the same as three jackhammers all going at once.

Erich Strom was one of those creatures who could concentrate no matter where he was. He reviewed things to make sure that everything was in order while Blackwell and Liesl watched across the darkened field for the other van—and Cruz . . . and two million dollars.

To some degree, Strom knew he had taken a chance by having Cruz pick up the cash alone.

But he did not really see Cruz taking a hike with the money—he was small potatoes—and it might have been a greater risk for either him or Liesl to show up. Maybe the pigs were double-dealing. They could have arrested him on the spot.

There was another reason why Cruz wouldn't do it. He knew that he and Liesl would never stop looking for him.

Their destination was Argentina, where he knew a few

important people and where it would be very easy to get into. It was the perfect place for people like him and Liesl. With two million dollars they could live like royalty for the rest of their lives.

Of course Strom had no intention of retiring. He was too young for that. And it would bore him.

No, he wouldn't retire. They drove cars in Argentina too.

Of course the ransom money would be numbered. But it could be laundered. He would launder it through a couple of Bahamian banks first, then Taiwanese, then Swiss.

He would have to pay, maybe 200 Gs. But he thought, $1.8 million was better than a poke in the scrotum with a sharp stick. He smiled inwardly.

The cops would be after him as well as the FBI and maybe some LA cops because their partners had been iced.

He would also have the wiseguys after him.

A pincers movement, but they wouldn't be able to touch him. Not in Argentina, not anywhere.

Anyway, Romano was small potatoes. Those wops weren't going to send some shooters halfway around the world for that dumb guinee. He doubted it, but he didn't care. It might be fun.

He joined Liesl and Blackwell looking across the field.

All the activity and life was at the far end of the field. There were planes disgorging passengers, planes taking off and landing, small carts and vans driving this way and that, and the myriad lights—the sodium lights, the blue and red runway lights, the lights of the large and small vehicles that drove around the airport providing this service or that.

They watched intently for a sign of the van. There was starting to be a tension in the air.

Then a vehicle seemed to be heading their way, its single-beam headlights on a beeline for the Falcon . . .

Liesl spotted it.

"Erich! Erich, he's here."

Quickly Strom and Liesl went down the hydraulic steps and waited for the van. It stopped a few yards from where Strom was standing.

Cruz got out the side door.

"Do you have it?" Strom asked.

Cruz reached back into the van and withdrew a black suitcase.

"It's all here."

"Good work," Strom said, and then pulled the H & K automatic from behind him. "And . . ."

"Mr. Strom, they're over . . ."

". . . good-bye," Strom added, and then shot Cruz twice in the face. He flopped to the ground and Strom opened the case.

It brimmed with cash.

Even the normally controlled Strom could not contain himself. He clutched a handful of bills and shook it over his head.

"Liesl!" he exhorted.

Then, out of the side of his eye, he became aware of a figure emerging from the back of the van. It was Nick Pulovski. He stopped.

He was in a combat stance, a .357 in his hands.

"Here's the interest, scumbag."

Strom was stunned, stunned at seeing Pulovski alive and stunned to see him here . . .

But he reacted quickly and brought the gun around instinctively and fired as Pulovski fired, his bullet smashing into Strom's shoulder and knocking him backward and the money flying from his hand like leaves in the wind and the suitcase hit the ground and part of the money was churned up into the air by the plane's props and Pulovski evaded Strom's fire and then a new threat: Liesl stood in the plane door with the Uzi and fired silently, peppering the asphalt as Pulovski scurried to evade and then Blackwell had the Falcon window up and started to blast away with a shotgun at Pulovski and then a new sound—tires screeching as Ackerman, gun out the window, burned rubber as he aimed the van for the Falcon and Liesl turned and spun and fired at Ackerman who got off two shots, both hitting Blackwell before his front window was shattered, then shoved the briefcase against the accelerator and dived onto the airstrip just before the van smashed into the front of the plane, spilling Liesl out of the doorway, down the steps, and onto the strip.

Pulovski, meanwhile, pinned by the fire, got up to fire again but was knocked down again as Strom, bleeding but alive, got up and emptied the rest of the clip at him.

Strom grabbed the partially filled case and he and Liesl ran away from the plane until they were swallowed by the darkness at the edge of the airstrip.

The entire exchange of gunfire had taken all of fifteen seconds, over one hundred rounds of ammunition had been fired and only two people—Strom and Blackwell—had been hit.

Ackerman, bruised by his rollout onto the airstrip, ran up to Pulovski and, as he did, watched perhaps one million dollars blow up and away like leaves.

"Another day, another dollar," Ackerman said.

Slowly, reassembling themselves, they started trotting in the direction of Strom and Liesl, and as they did they passed the air courier, the front of which looked like it had collided with an airplane.

"You didn't have to total the goddamn thing."

"What's the matter, speed racer . . . been behind the wheel so long you can't hoof it?"

Pulovski gave Ackerman one of his what-enormous-nostril-did-you-crawl-out-of looks and then they were off at almost a full run.

Ackerman was surprised. Pulovski was not Carl Lewis,

but he could pick 'em up and lay 'em down, and ran at a smooth, even pace that Ackerman had to struggle to keep up with.

Then Liesl tried to discourage pursuit with a burst from the Uzi, and they hit the turf.

"Lousy bitch," Ackerman said.

"Hell, I've had worse."

"I don't doubt it."

From a pocket Pulovski pulled a Beretta and fired three times, missing all three times. Then they were up running after them again.

Then, from behind, a terrible, huge rumbling sound and they turned and saw the specter of the Falcon 20, indeed appearing like a huge savage bird, bearing down on them across the grass, and inside the plane Blackwell, almost history, bleeding like a faucet, leaning heavily on the controls, his last act on earth a determination to take those two motherfuckers with him . . .

Ackerman and Pulovski stood directly in its path, the lights impaling them, pinning them to the grass. And just at the last moment Pulovski screamed, "Both sides, kid! Move it!"

They moved it, but Blackwell still had some reflexes left and he swerved the wheel hard to the right, the side Ackerman was on, and the wheel missed him by a hair and then he continued in a frenzied, demented, almost-Keystone Kops turn trying to run Ackerman down.

Ackerman ran for his life, but the weaker the blood loss made Blackwell, the more determined he became. And now, far away, Strom and Liesl ran along the airstrip, then cut across the grass toward the terminal buildings, and were lit up by the lights of an immense descending 767 jetliner.

Then Blackwell swung the plane again, and this time was almost for sure going to run over Ackerman when Pulovski appeared, and this time fired the .357 and the bullets punched out the glass over Blackwell's head and the airplane just missed Ackerman, and screeched and chewed up grass and burned rubber as it stopped on the airstrip.

Time stood still as, suddenly, Ackerman and Pulovski were frozen by a horrific sight. The Falcon was on the strip that was directly in the path of the 767, flaps down, lights blazing, close to touchdown . . .

And it touched down twenty yards from Blackwell who, in the cockpit, recognized the ear-shattering sound of engines in reverse thrust, and then light filled the cockpit like day and the plane impacted with the Falcon as if it wasn't there, shredding the fifty-three-foot plane as if it were made of Styrofoam, and the reverse thrust continued until the 767 skidded off the runway onto the grass and stopped.

Immediately there was the distant clang of firebells but no fire . . .

And then Pulovski turned toward the terminal buildings and it all came to him . . . just like that, a memory of Billy dead on the fucking street and him dead, too, his life as a cop a piece of excrement that never went anywhere but, goddammit, it would go somewhere now. This was his one shot to do it all, and it would probably never come again and he somehow knew that he would do it in those buildings, or he would die like Billy, and that is the way it was going to be and that was okay. He had a shot, and that's all he wanted.

His eyes glittered, hard and bright, his jaw muscles jumped.

"C'mon, kid, let's get these assholes."

"You got it," his partner said.

CHAPTER
41

STROM and Liesl ran past a docking 747 through an immense opening into baggage unloading, an area in which beauty wasn't even given an afterthought by the architect. It was gray with metal framework, pipes, cables, wires, and all manner of stuff running along the ceiling as well as hanging fluorescent lights that cast a cold light on the proceedings below.

And it had a strong smell of kerosene, jet fuel, which took a while to get used to.

The area was busy. Beefy little cars called tugs were pulling big two-level carts on which were piled stacks of luggage, as well as boxy, silvery luggage containers, and men were unloading other carts, tossing the luggage either on moving carousels or down chutes where it would feed onto carousels that went to the main terminal where the passengers picked up their luggage a level below.

It was, in essence, a kind of controlled chaos . . . which

Strom liked. He and Liesl could get away more easily; no one would likely question why they were there, which could lead to more confrontation.

They started across toward the terminal doors.

Almost as quickly they were separated by a hard-driving tug and a line of luggage carts, and there was no getting back. Looking back toward the entrance Strom—and Liesl—saw Pulovski.

Liesl went one way and Strom ducked down behind one of the baggage containers strewn about as Pulovski angled for a clear shot.

He fired just as Strom got behind cover and the result was predictable: it cleared the area of people with the same effect that turning on the lights in a roach-infested kitchen would have on the roaches.

A moment later Ackerman arrived and took up a position behind Pulovski.

Pulovski spoke, his voice whispery, cold. "Strom is mine."

Ackerman caught sight of Liesl as she disappeared into a hallway and made his way behind some baggage carriers until he could get to the corridor.

Meanwhile, Pulovski started to move toward Strom—an action greeted with a bullet that smashed perilously close to his head.

He waited a few seconds, then cautiously looked up and stood up, keeping his body covered.

Strom was nowhere to be seen.

Liesl knew that she was running for her life, and she ran like that, bowling over people who got in her way. Ackerman, gun in hand, ran after her . . .

Out of the hall, she ran down a crowded corridor that connected two terminals, three long moving sidewalk ramps stretched from one end of the corridor to the other, and she stepped onto one of the ramps, still pushing her way forward.

Ackerman was gaining, but he didn't know it. He couldn't see her. All he could see, far ahead, was commotion.

He leapt up onto the divider between the ramps and then he saw her, bursting out of the corridor into the crowded terminal. He raced along the divider, people screaming and ducking as he did.

God, he thought, of all the places . . . and she didn't give a shit. She had a fucking Uzi. She'd kill anyone who got in her way, or happened to be there by accident.

Ackerman reached the end of the corridor.

The terminal was crowded, just like he thought it would be. He spotted her about thirty yards away—and she him. She raised the Uzi and fired a burst just as he dove out of the way, coming up behind a row of empty seats.

There was instant bedlam, people screaming, diving out of the way. Ackerman couldn't get a clear shot, and then he saw two uniformed security guards approach her.

"Hold it!" one of them said. "Stop right there."

Liesl's answer was to try to gun them down in cold blood, but they jumped out of the way and she only wounded one.

For just that moment, she had been distracted.

And it was all Ackerman needed.

From the side of her eye she sensed something . . . and Ackerman moved partly out from a support pillar.

"Freeze."

But Liesl didn't freeze. She spun around, Uzi raised, and David Ackerman had his Beretta about level with her nostrils.

"Amateur," he said, and pulled the trigger.

Her head snapped back and she was knocked to the floor, dead.

Ackerman walked over to the body and looked at her in the same way he might look at dogshit.

In the baggage unloading area Nick Pulovski was moving carefully and cautiously from one baggage container to the next.

He knew how dangerous Strom was.

Maybe, he thought, Strom had gotten out. Maybe . . .

Pulovski moved into the open momentarily—and a shot rang out, again barely missing him.

And maybe, Pulovski thought, he didn't.

Pulovski dropped to the floor behind a tug and caught sight of moving, booted feet showing beneath a cart. Slowly and carefully he climbed into the tug, his back shielded by the machine.

He reached up and manipulated the rearview mirror, scanning the entire area . . .

And caught sight of Strom about thirty yards away, moving from one storage container to another.

The conveyor belt, loaded with baggage, was moving in Strom's direction and then toward an opening in the wall out of sight.

Pulovski had an idea.

He took one more look, then exposed himself to fire and hunched down behind a large bag on the conveyor belt and moved along with it, out of sight . . . he hoped.

Then, five seconds later he saw Strom but Strom didn't see him and he leveled the .357 at Strom's back—but just like that Strom, like some predatory animal sensing danger, had turned and was firing at Pulovski, the slugs slamming into luggage, and again Pulovski couldn't get a clear shot at him . . .

Then there was silence for a few seconds that is an eternity in a gunfight and Pulovski looked; Strom was gone, and Pulovski didn't know where . . .

He started back from the way he came, crouched, gun ready, checking behind everything and at one point passed two baggage handlers, who were trying to make themselves part of the concrete.

Pulovski whispered, "Just stay down."

Where the fuck is this hump, he thought. Where are you, asshole?

An engine roared to life—and Pulovski was suddenly aware that a tug was bearing down on him—and the handlers.

"Move it," he shouted, "get out of the way!"

They did and so did Pulovski and the tug crashed heavily into a luggage carrier behind him.

He looked at the carrier. The seat was smeared with blood, but no Strom.

Where the fuck was he, he thought.

From behind him, Strom spoke, a single chilling word: "Good-bye."

Pulovski reacted instinctively, whirling around as Strom pulled the trigger, and Pulovski felt the bullet plow into his belly, a hot wire, and he fired and hit Strom, the force knocking him ass over teakettle headfirst down a baggage chute . . . which emerged on a carousel in the terminal, his body askew, people who thought the excitement was over screaming anew . . .

And then David Ackerman was there, near Strom, who still had life left in him and fired at Ackerman, hitting him in the leg, sending him heavily to the hard white tile floor.

Strom got up. He walked over and picked up Ackerman's gun. Ackerman was helpless.

"Your luck," Strom said, feeling a surge of power, "has just ended."

He took aim . . .

And from behind came a shout: "Strom!"

It was Pulovski, who, in combat firing position, squeezed

off a round, but heard the sound that was the dread of police officers everywhere: click.

He was out of bullets, and Strom laughed, raised his gun to finish this troublesome bastard off, but Ackerman, meanwhile, had one final card—a card, one of many, he learned from Pulovski—and he reached down and pulled a .22 out of an ankle holster and squeezed off rapid fire at Strom, who went down, his gun clattering to the floor.

Strom laid there, leaking, and Pulovski, his stomach bleeding fairly heavily, came over to him. Strom, ever the snake, reached for his gun, and Pulovski stepped on his wrist.

Pulovski looked down at him.

"You'd better . . . call an ambulance . . . cop."

Pulovski's face was hard, and he had death in his eyes.

He reached down and parted Strom's bloodied shirt, located the silver bullet and ripped it off.

He loaded it into the .357.

"There must be," he said, and had a quick, terrible image of Billy Parker lying on the street, "a hundred good reasons why I shouldn't blow your brains out, scumbag . . ."

Pulovski took his foot off Strom's wrist.

". . . but now I can't think of one."

Strom understood and his face contorted, finally, in fear.

Pulovski pulled the trigger and put Strom's brains on the tile.

Two minutes later Pulovski and Ackerman were sitting on the floor together. Pulovski was holding his gut, in deep pain. But Pulovski was Pulovski.

"Looks like you owe me a cigar, kid."

Ackerman reached into his jacket and pulled out a cigar, badly bent but otherwise intact. He stripped off the cellophane and handed Pulovski the cigar.

"My brand . . . where'd you get this?"

"Your house. I picked it up the same time I borrowed your bike."

Pulovski's eyes narrowed considerably.

"It's nothing I can't fix," Ackerman said.

Pulovski, growing whiter by the moment, broke the cigar in half and stuck one half in his mouth.

"Well, kid, since you're so handy, why don't you fix me up with a light?"

Ackerman searched through his pockets. No light. He looked at Pulovski, who was starting to lose consciousness.

"Some things never fuckin' change . . ."

And the cigar fell from his mouth and he lost consciousness.

CHAPTER
42

A MONTH later David Ackerman, limping slightly, walked down the same precinct corridor that Pulovski had a month after Parker had been killed.

Other cops commiserated with him as they passed him by.

"Hey, man," one said, "it's too bad about Nick, isn't it?"

And another: "I always told him it was gonna happen someday."

"It's a helluva way to end," said yet another.

And Ackerman nodded, but he didn't know what the hell they were talking about. Nick was alive—and out of hospital.

Then he entered the bullpen area and threaded his way through desks to the lieutenant's office, having to pass Cheech and Chong, aka Lance and Wang, who looked like they wanted to draw down on him.

He smiled pleasantly.

Ackerman walked in and was surprised; instead of Ray

Garcia, Nick Pulovski was sitting behind the lieutenant's desk.

"Nick . . . where's the lieutenant?"

"You're looking at him."

"You? What happened to Lieutenant Garcia?"

"*Captain* Garcia. Got kicked upstairs. You got a problem with that, Ackerman?"

Now Ackerman understood what other cops were saying: Poor Pulovski had become a boss.

"No . . . I'm just thinking you look pretty good sitting there behind that desk, Nick."

Pulovski put a foot on the desk and pulled his flask from his ankle holster.

"That's *Lieutenant* Pulovski to you, kid, unless you want to find yourself on parking meter duty. *Capish?*"

Ackerman *capish*ed and watched Nick add a little flavoring to his coffee.

Ackerman spotted a box of donuts on the desk and picked out the kind Pulovski hated.

"Never far from your thoughts, am I?" Ackerman said.

"My nightmares is more like it . . . furthermore, kid, if I ever find that bike in my spot again I'm gonna have the damn thing impounded . . . speaking of which get your ass off my desk and park it elsewhere."

Ackerman got up and munched his donut.

"You know, Nick . . . Lieutenant, I ran a make on that asshole we've been seeing all over and it turns out to be . . ."

Ackerman was distracted. He turned. A serious-looking young woman, neatly dressed and coiffed, had stepped into the office.

"Who the . . . hey, listen, this is private, okay?"

"No," Pulovski said, "this is Heather Torres."

"Heather Torres?" Ackerman said, walking up to her and escorting her out the door. "*Nice* to meet you, Heather."

"Ackerman," Pulovski said.

Ackerman turned.

"That was your new partner."

Ackerman blinked and turned back. Heather's face was red . . . and Ackerman understood.

"What are you," Pulovski said, "some kind of chauvinist? I went over Torres's records—her test scores are better'n yours were. She's perfect."

Ackerman looked at her up and down.

"Oh, yeah," he said, "then why's her shield upside down?"

Heather, panicked, glanced down and reddened some more, realizing she'd been had.

Ackerman walked over and peeked in behind her suit jacket at her waist.

Just as he suspected. He took the belt off and said, "Get a shoulder holster."

Pulovski nodded and put a mangled cheroot in his mouth. He searched his desk for a moment.

Ackerman reached into his pocket, pulled out a lighter, and tossed it to Pulovski. He lit the cigar and took a satisfying puff.

"Keep it," Ackerman said.

Pulovski pocketed the lighter.

"Well," Pulovski said, "what are you two standing around here for . . . go arrest somebody or something."

They started to leave, and then Ackerman looked back and his eyes and Pulovski's met. It was a moment of warmth, affection, respect, but never stated, as close as the cop code would allow.

Then they were gone out the door.

Wang began Heather Torres's ordeal. He stood up and patted her on the back and handed her a napkin.

"Looks a little wet behind those ears this morning, honey. Thought you could use this."

His equally compassionate partner, Lance, joined in.

"Hey, Ackerman, you know what they say about these virgins, don't . . ."

"Yeah, yeah I know all about it."

They continued to walk to the door, the room tittering as they did. On Heather's back was a sign Wang had placed there: "I WANT YOUR SEX."

Just before they exited, Ackerman reached over, peeled the sign off without Heather knowing, crumpled it and dropped it on the floor, and they disappeared out the doorway. Ackerman . . . and the rookie.

By the year 2000, 2 out of 3 Americans could be illiterate.

It's true.

Today, 75 million adults… about one American in three, can't read adequately. And by the year 2000, U.S. News & World Report envisions an America with a literacy rate of only 30%.

Before that America comes to be, you can stop it… by joining the fight against illiteracy today.

Call the Coalition for Literacy at toll-free **1-800-228-8813** and volunteer.

Volunteer Against Illiteracy. The only degree you need is a degree of caring.

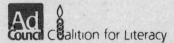

Ad Council C:alition for Literacy

Warner Books is proud to be an active supporter of the Coalition for Literacy.